"There isn't a man here who could quicken my heartbeat!"

Juliana was flushed with anger. "You warned me not to cause havoc with your presumably women-hungry men up here...now let me warn *you*. You're to leave me alone to enjoy my own peaceful existence. I'm not looking for any romantic interludes to give a fillip to living in isolation. My pulses don't stir so easily. Do I make myself clear"

She turned to sweep out of the office, aware it was a good exit line. Tulloch's chair scraped back. She was tall enough herself, but he towered over her. His hands shot out and grasped her wrists in a grip that bruised.

"Very clear, Miss Hendrie. Except that the lady doth protest too much. I don't believe a word of it!"

Books by Essie Summers

HARLEQUIN ROMANCE

These books may be available at your local bookseller.

Don't miss any of our special offers. Write to us at the following address for information on our newest releases.

Harlequin Reader Service
P.O. Box 52040, Phoenix, AZ 85072-2040
Canadian address: P.O. Box 2800, Postal Station A,
5170 Yonge St., Willowdale, Ont. M2N 6J3

Winter in July

Essie Summers

Harlequin Books

TORONTO • NEW YORK • LONDON
AMSTERDAM • PARIS • SYDNEY • HAMBURG
STOCKHOLM • ATHENS • TOKYO • MILAN

Original hardcover edition published in 1984
by Mills & Boon Limited

ISBN 0-373-02688-9

Harlequin Romance first edition April 1985

This book is dedicated to the memory of my father, Edwin Summers, who in a way, inspired it when I was twelve. He rented a seaside cottage at Pleasant Point, near Christchurch that year and I discovered some very ancient magazines, in one of which was a poem I loved on an English July, and I can't give the poet's name, unfortunately. My father had left his loved Northumberland one July thirteen years before, and the year after, to the day and the hour, I was born in an Antipodean July, in a howling snowstorm. When he read the poem, he suggested I write one to match, in praise of a winter July. I didn't keep a copy of either, but, like most writers, have a long memory and both poems came back to me, I hope accurately. So here they are, Dad, in a permanent form in this novel of the Canterbury you came to love so well.

— With love

From Essie.

CHAPTER ONE

JULIANA HENDRIE stared at the man she'd met only seconds before. Could she be hearing aright? 'I beg your pardon! What on earth can occasion an attitude like this? Everyone else has made me feel I'm only a degree lower than a heroine to accompany a man to an area as remote as Thor's Hill . . . the very back of beyond!'

As he went to speak she held up a hand. 'Oh, don't mistake that for vanity. *I* don't regard myself as a heroine—I'm just going by other people's reactions. You appear to be the only one out of step. And in any case, why should *you* feel you have the say-so, Mr MacNair? My patient owns the station. Or can I possibly have made a mistake? Isn't it up to him to say whom he employs?'

The man the Almoner had introduced to her in the semi-privacy of the ward kitchen remained quite unmoved by this outburst. 'I think that not being a New Zealander you've got too formal an idea of relationships on our rural scene. I'm the manager and therefore the one responsible for the welfare of every person on the estate. I think you've allowed yourself to be swayed by Mr Ramsay's natural longing to be back in the environment he's known all his life. I would have thought a trained Sister wouldn't have allowed herself to be so involved with one particular patient. We have a house at Fairlie, where George could have instant access to the doctor. He and Mrs Ramsay could have stayed there. But you've encouraged him to dare the isolation. I find it poor.'

The eyes under Sister Hendrie's starched veil flashed emerald fire. 'I make allowances for the fact that you've just arrived from this isolated region, Mr MacNair. Mrs Ramsay did her best and came to me in despair. He said *nothing* was going to stop him going back home, that even if he were going to die he'd die among his

7

mountains, though he'd no intention of shuffling off
this mortal coil yet, life was too darned interesting!
When she knew she couldn't move him, and heard that
I was moving on, with only a long holiday spell ahead
of me, she begged me to come with them—said it would
restrain George from too much folly up there, if I
came.'

He uttered an indescribable sound of contempt. 'How
ridiculous! If Grizel can't manage him, how could you?
I never——'

Again he was checked by the upheld hand. 'I don't
think you know much about the nursing profession.'
The hand plucked at her white bodice. 'This, to a nurse,
is like uniform to a soldier. It gives authority. I've seen
many a wilful male patient scuttling back into bed at
the order of a girl of eighteen, when not all the pleas of
a wife could have persuaded him. At times I find your
sex very childish, Mr MacNair, and as quick to respond
to sensible authority. In view of your opposition, I'd
love to tell you I'd prefer to go on holiday rather than
come to Thor's Hill on duty, but I'd despise myself for
behaving like a thwarted six-year-old.'

The craggily built man confronting her considered
that, tawny brows down, mouth set in a straight line.
Then, 'Before you make up your mind completely,
you'd better know what you're heading into. It's the
roughest of all New Zealand terrain. Once you cross the
Rubicon, you can be cut off from any swift return if
you can't take it.'

Juliana made an impatient and contemptuous gesture
herself. 'Aren't you being unnecessarily dramatic?
Crossing the Rubicon indeed! I know the Whakarite
isn't bridged, Mrs Ramsay told me, but——'

He smiled derisively, 'You must buy yourself a
dictionary of Maori place-names, Sister. Whakarite
means the act of decision and the dictionary gives the
English rendering of it as "The Rubicon . . . to take an
irrevocable step." So often, at any season, that river
makes it *impossible* to return.'

She managed to control her chagrin and said, 'Sorry,
I didn't know it had so literal a translation. However,

for Mrs Ramsay's peace of mind, if Mr Ramsay is so determined to go home, that's all the more reason for a trained nurse to be in attendance. If the thought of my salary adding to the payroll daunts you, perhaps Mr Ramsay hasn't told you that as I was contemplating a holiday at Lake Tekapo and Mount Cook, I'm taking only my keep, refusing wages.'

For the first time he looked disconcerted. 'I don't know if we could allow that—if you come.'

'It doesn't rest with you. It's all agreed. Now, if you don't mind, I'm off duty in twenty minutes and I've a great deal to do between then and leaving tomorrow at noon, for Fairlie, with Mr and Mrs Ramsay. As you'll know, she hired a car to go up to Ashburton to see a friend. I need the time to set the flat in order for the next occupant and to prepare for a little send-off some of the staff are giving me tonight.'

His lip curled. 'Better make the most of that party. You won't have that kind of social life way back in the big fellows. Mountains can be both enclosing and intimidating, you know.' He paused, then added, 'The whole thing is absurd. You came to New Zealand from a famous London hospital, I know, because George said so. You'd have been better to have stuck to nursing in Auckland or Christchurch—more your own terrain. Our line of country could scare the hell out of you.'

The green eyes met his with laughter in them, mocking him. 'I doubt it. The London hospital wasn't my background, though, it was only part of my training-ground. I was born and brought up in the Scottish Highlands.'

He ought to have been abashed. Instead he said, a matching amusement in his eyes, 'Can you really compare the mountains of Scotland with our Southern Alps?'

'Not in height, but if you should ever climb among them you just might regard them with some awe. They have hazards too. They're not to be despised.'

'I do know them,' he told her. 'I visited where my forebears came from, and did a lot of climbing there.'

Juliana thought for a moment. 'MacNair—oh, yes,

around Loch Awe, I presume. Very pleasant, well peopled, with delightful villages and fishing inns. I can understand your opinion of our mountains, then. But we were much farther north.'

'I daresay it's more lonely, more wild, but not to be compared with the heart-chilling isolation of our high country stations ... Thor's Hill, Dragonshill, Craigievar, and Heronscrag. True Alpine stuff.'

'Sounds intriguing,' she agreed. 'But now I really must get on. Mind if I request something? Don't take this as personal, it's merely professional concern for my patient. Please don't let Mr Ramsay have any idea that you're opposed to my accompanying him. An undisturbed mind is a desirable ingredient in convalescence.'

He looked at her without speaking momentarily. Perhaps subduing anger? Then, 'Do you really think I'd be small-minded enough to disturb this man to whom I owe so much? Seeing I've taken that from you, who've known George Ramsay only a few weeks, will you take this from me? You've a journey of a day and a half ahead of you. For your patient's sake, don't make it too late a night. Hangovers and crossing the Rubicon don't mix.'

He'd turned on his heel and gone before she could subdue her ire to a cool answer.

Some hours later, setting out early refreshments for the nurses who had not been on duty, Juliana suddenly wanted to giggle. If Mr MacNair ... High-and-Mightiness MacNair ... could only see this gathering, not a man in sight, and Matron sitting in the midst of her girls! At that moment the bell rang.

Juliana turned, a tray of cups in her hands. 'Was there anyone coming later? Marjorie, how about you answering the door?'

The next moment she almost dropped the tray as she heard first Marjorie's voice, 'Who shall I say?' and a deep answering one, 'Tulloch MacNair from Thor's Hill.'

Tulloch! What a perfect name for that weatherbeaten

man from the Mackenzie area ... Tulloch of the Tussocks! What on earth was he doing here? Immediately she was aware of the feminine interest riveted on this caller. She must not allow any hint of hostility to creep into her tone. She said sweetly, 'Oh, how nice that you called in, Mr MacNair. You're just in time for supper. Some of the nurses are on early duty tomorrow, so we're not making it a late sitting. You'll never remember the names, but I'll introduce you just the same. This is Matron, or rather Head Nurse, as they now call it in New Zealand. So, Mrs Satterthwaite ... and this ...'

She sat him next to the Matron and took malicious amusement in hearing Mrs Satterthwaite tell him how lucky he was and to sing her praises. He was surprisingly easy among them, and the way he tucked into the food one would have suspected he'd had only a snack dinner. Maddie Soames said, biting into the hot chicken patties, 'Aren't you a fortunate man? If your cook takes off, as I believe they have a habit of doing on these remote stations, you'll be able to press Juliana into service. I hope Juliana doesn't think it's cupboard love with us, but we sure have enjoyed our get-togethers in her flat. We all love home cooking after our institution meals.'

'They're certainly good,' said Tulloch MacNair, reaching out for another savoury. 'In years past we've had emergencies on the cooking front, but the cook we've got now has been with us for years, and he's a gem. Mrs Ramsay cooks for the homestead, of course, Willocks is in the cookhouse, but the men of the household help Grizel with some chores—seasonal stuff, when we come back, say, with dozens of cases of fruit and vegetables for the deep-freezes. But never fear, Miss Hendrie, we won't look on you as a dogsbody. We know your job is to get that stubborn George Ramsay back to full health and strength so you can continue with your New Zealand touring.'

Very neat, that, putting a term on her stay. In another three-quarters of an hour the girls were leaving. They'd offered to wash up, but Tulloch MacNair, with unbelievable cheek, had said, 'In view of all that early duty some of you face, I'm sure Sister Hendrie will permit her new employer to wield a tea-towel. Regard me as a bonus to your night off, girls.'

He had certainly been a great success with the nurses. She could have shot him! When the last goodnight had been said Juliana said coldly, 'That wasn't at all necessary.'

He said blandly, 'What wasn't?'

'Staying on. You've seen what you came for ... and you must be satisfied it wasn't a wild party. Nothing but a sherry and coffee. Not a doctor or an intern in sight, just a gathering of workmates.'

The tawny brows shot up. 'What motives you impute to me! I merely came to tell you that I've heard from Grizel and she's leaving Ashburton at eight, so we hope to get away at ten-thirty instead of noon. I thought you'd need notice of that. When I rang the hospital they told me this flat wasn't on the phone as it's used mostly for temporary staff, but gave me your address, and I saw it was quite near my motel. My apologies, anyway, for thinking you might throw a wild party on your last night.'

She looked slightly mollified. 'Thank you. One doesn't like to be misjudged. But why didn't you just say your piece and leave with the others? That mightn't sound hospitable, but I was really keen to have a reasonably early night.'

He shrugged. 'Might as well come out with it. I didn't want to bring this up in the ward kitchen—it's not private enough. It's just that ...'

His hesitation made her nervous. She said abruptly, 'Come on, don't hesitate. You were brutally frank this morning. I can take anything from you after that. I realise you're a blunt man.'

His glance was searching. 'Well, finding this innocuous gathering tonight almost made me think it needn't be said, but perhaps it'll be for the best. We live very closely together up there in the somewhat restricted atmosphere of the station. Naturally, we can't get away from each other, so emotions can get out of hand. There's so little variety in social contacts. We've had governesses for the shepherds' children who've played the Old Harry with the men's feelings. If you'd been in your late forties and as plain as a pikestaff, it might have been different, but to strike an ash-blonde with green eyes and more than a bit of allure is a bit much. To say nothing of old George being positively besotted with you!' He paused and added, 'So I thought if I came round I could ask you to go easy on our men ... and old George.'

Juliana turned away swiftly, swallowed, put her hands on the table to steady herself, draw in some deep breaths, then swung back. 'Mr MacNair, I'm finding it hard to control my temper. I don't often lose it, but I can. You really deserve that I should smack your face! I find this ridiculous. I've never, ever, been regarded as—as a siren before. For one thing, they don't usually come freckled. None of your men will be in danger from me. I won't be staying long, as you've been at pains to point out. But there's something I like even less ... your saying Mr Ramsay is *besotted*. That's perfectly stupid. Patients often get quite fond of their nurses and forget them the moment they leave hospital. As for Mr Ramsay, think of his age. For another, he's a married man!'

His eyes widened. 'He's a widower. Didn't he tell you? Perfectly free ... and I've seen many a man his age make a fool of himself over a pretty face.'

Her eyes were even more startled. 'A widower? But what about Grizel? Mrs Ramsay? You've surely——'

'Grizel's his sister. There's no likeness, I know, with him so fair and her so dark. It sometimes happens. But you must have known.'

'I met her as Mrs Ramsay. How come——'

'She married another Ramsay, no connection at all. It can happen. Her husband died not long after George lost Polly. He was a minister and died while in a parish, so she had no home of her own. Their children were all married, so she simply came back to her childhood home to housekeep for George. I was sure you'd know, as you've nursed him so long and he's not a reticent man.'

'I wasn't specialling him, though,' she explained. 'I had other patients under my care, and she was introduced as Mrs Ramsay, not as his sister. It was only during the last week or two that I had much to do with him in a personal way. He asked about my plans when he knew I was on a working holiday and I said they took in Mount Cook. He got it into his head that if I came up to Thor's Hill, they wouldn't insist on convalescing at Fairlie. Mrs Ramsay was really keen. She was terrified he'd go right home whether I was with them or not. Patients can get the most deadly homesickness, and it's wonderful how quickly they recover in their own surroundings, given the chance, and expert care. I can promise you there'll be no repercussions with your men!' Suddenly she giggled, wrinkling up her nose and a dimple appearing. 'This is entirely a new experience for me, being regarded as a dangerous woman. Most of the time I feel very much Sister Hendrie and quite a bit older than some of my nurses . . . my mother will be most amused. She, now, still regards me as her madcap, tomboy daughter!'

He stared. As she giggled, the image of the ashy blonde fled and instead was a freckle-nosed, mischievous girl. He felt disconcerted. To cover up he said, 'Where is your mother? In Scotland?'

She hesitated too, she must resist the temptation to score off this man. It would never do to say that Mother and Dad were at this very moment among some of the highest mountains in the world, in the Himalayas. Instead she said, 'They're touring Asia. I didn't want to go with them, I've always yearned to see New Zealand.'

The man lost his hostile look. 'Any particular reason?'

'Yes. My father is—was—a New Zealander. But he's lived in Scotland longer than he lived here.'

'Didn't he want to return to the scenes of his boyhood with you?'

'No, he's never seemed to want to come back. He wasn't very happy here. He lost his parents when very young, and hadn't another relation in the world.'

(Not that that was the only reason he'd never expressed any nostalgia, she was sure of that. And his reluctance to come was the reason she was here. She had a burning compulsion to know why.)

Tulloch MacNair nodded. 'I can understand that. A tough childhood could make for a lack of nostalgic feelings. Where did he live?'

'Somewhere in Canterbury,' she said carelessly. 'His foster-parents were rootless people and moved from place to place.' Like a lightning flash she wondered what this man would say if she had replied: 'He was a young shepherd on Thor's Hill.'

A silence fell between them. She looked at him pointedly. He said, 'Yes, must be going. Have you much stuff to take?'

'Not really. I'm used to travelling. My father's work takes him to many places, so he trained us to travel light. But I never can resist buying books, so I've a carton of those. Apart from that, two suitcases and a weekend bag.' There was one lot of stuff she wouldn't mention, stowed in her wardrobe. Time for him to find out tomorrow that she wasn't entirely a greenhorn in the areas of snow and ice.

When she was in bed, inevitably Juliana's mind roved to the moment when she'd found out that the star patient in her ward owned the very sheep station where her father had worked. Till then she'd only known it was in the Alpine region. It had come about from an idle remark that might never have been made.

She'd said, waving a hand at the window where a rooftop glittered with frost, 'I find it so hard to believe it's mid-June. By the calendar I feel that the fences should be smothered with roses, and lavender and mignonette scenting the air. Instead, they'll bloom here in December. This makes me realise I'm in the Southern Hemisphere.'

The other patients in the four-bed ward had listened too, and George Ramsay had chuckled. 'Aye, long ago we had an old Scots shepherd who said he'd never got used to our topsy-turvy world down under ...

Christmas in summer, Easter in autumn, and spring in September. He reckoned July and August when sometimes, among the Alps, we saw only snow, with no ground showing if the falls had been heavy, seemed quite unreal to him. He got a very ancient magazine he'd found in his quarters one night, and said, "This is what July ought to be like." There was summat about that evening I've never forgotten—made me realise as never before that our pioneers not only had to cope with change of environment but also opposite seasons. The plants and saplings took the change better than they did. When the summer suns gave place to autumn, they obligingly adapted and turned gold and russet and in one short year became acclimatised.

'He read us this poem he'd found. I remember it began: "Sing glory of summer, July with her riot of vines and sweet briars ..." and so on. It was the essence of an English Summer. Sister, what's the matter?'

Juliana hadn't realised she'd gasped. She said hurriedly, 'Nothing really, Mr Ramsay ... just that I thought it sounded familiar.'

George had shaken his head very decidedly. 'I doubt you'd ever have come across it. It wasn't in an anthology or anything, just in a tattered magazine that was well out of date even when our old shepherd discovered it. I reckon it went back to the twenties. The reason it stuck in my mind is because we had a laddie on the station belonging to the married couple. A bright, adventurous boy. He wasn't theirs, they'd adopted him when his parents died. He did correspondence lessons with our girls—had a flair for writing poetry. I said to him why didn't he write a poem to match it, of a New Zealand July among the Alps. He did, and it was included in the magazine of the Correspondence School at the end of the year.

'We were very proud of it. I got him to print us a copy of both poems, side by side, and we had it framed. I'd said to him, "You can't very well start it the same way, Todd, you can't sing glory of winter." I can see him yet, eyes alight. "Oh, yes, I can, Mr Ramsay, I like winter best here." He did too. Never saw such a kid for the snow! I wished I'd had a son like that. When they went down to Fairlie with the girls for a few weeks of mixing at the school there, he was always homesick.'

Juliana had closed her eyes momentarily against the shock of the revelation. Todd ... *of course*. Dad's nickname for his second name. The couple who'd adopted him had given him their surname and when they had died and couldn't be hurt by his action, he'd had it changed back to his own. Not Todd Powers any longer, but Fergus Talbot Hendrie.

Juliana wanted to hold this moment fast, to prolong it as much as possible. 'Can you remember the poem, Mr Ramsay?' she asked. 'Or is it too long?'

(She knew it was short. She just didn't want to give away the fact that she'd known it from childhood, reading it as one of Dad's earliest poems, in his little old scrapbook.)

George thought for a moment, flattered by the interest, then his face cleared. 'My memory's not as bad as I thought. I reckon I can remember them both.'

Juliana knew she'd never forget this moment. George began:

> *'Sing glory of Summer, July with her riot,*
> *Of vines and sweet briars; July with her quiet;*
> *July with her fires of poppy and rose,*
> *July with her close, clinging bees in the clover,*
> *July the gay weaver, the rover, the lover;*
> *July the bright daughter of delicate June,*
> *July with her moon, at the full like a jewel,*
> *July who is cruel alone when she leaves us*
> *And flies and bereaves us ... glad, golden July.'*

Sister Hendrie, eyes alight, prompted him, 'And ... the New Zealand one, please?'

George's voice trembled for a moment. She loved him for that. He said, 'This is what little Todd wrote:

> *'Sing glory of Winter, July with her chalice*
> *A-brimming with hailstones, each stinging with malice;*

July with her sunsets aflame on the snows,
July with her dawnings of coral and rose;
July with her rainbows that straddle the mountains,
Her icicles frozen like crystal-hard fountains;
July the bright daughter of half-hearted June,
July with her moon at the full like a jewel,
July who is cruel alone when she leaves us
And flies and bereaves us, wild, stormy July.'

George had sighed. 'Aye, Todd Powers was an engaging little chap. I'd have liked fine to know what he made of himself.'

Juliana was surprised to hear her voice sound so matter-of-fact. 'Did you never know? Did they move away and lose touch?'

'They moved shortly after he wrote that poem. He was only twelve then. We were thrilled when Todd came back to Thor's Hill when he was eighteen, as a shepherd. The Powers couple had died. They weren't young when they took him. We had great hopes of young Todd. But things went awry . . . he left the area. My wife grieved about him for a long time. She worried in case he went to the bad. I hope he didn't, but I don't think he would. He had promise and in many ways he had a raw deal out of life.'

At that moment the dinners arrived and all was stir and bustle. But when, later, George Ramsay asked her to accompany them to Thor's Hill, Juliana had taken it as a sign she was meant to go, to find out what had taken her father from those mountains he had undoubtedly loved, to climb other mountains on the far side of the world. Tomorrow she would be on her way, but nobody must know in case there was something that would reflect on her father's reputation, that father who was by now a world figure on the mountaineering scene. Juliana slept.

Grizel had arrived in good time, evidently, for they appeared before ten-thirty to pick Juliana up before getting George from the hospital. They had a Holden estate car, the back of it well packed but with room for

Juliana's luggage. She said, 'There's an extra item of luggage I didn't show you last night. It was stowed in my wardrobe, and I haven't wrapped it. I thought they'd slide in better not wrapped. Skis.'

They measured glances. Tulloch MacNair said, 'I rather suspect you're trying to score off me. I was somewhat scathing last night about our conditions, and this is your answer.'

It flicked her on the raw. 'Oh, you weren't *somewhat* scathing. You were *very* scathing. And whether I told you then or now would have made no difference. You'd still have felt I scored off you.'

To her surprise he nodded, even twinkled. 'Probably. I admit that. However, it's not just a glorified ski-field at Thor's Hill, but if you're at all proficient, we could use you snow-raking for sheep if you're game. We've had so little snow this year as yet it's bound to come.' He added, 'Snow-raking means digging out sheep buried in huge snowdrifts and under overhangs. Where did you ski? Kingussie?'

Was there a hint of patronage in his tone? She forbore to mention the ski-runs of Switzerland she'd known so well, from her childhood holidays with her grandmother. He'd take it for another score-off, and it could disturb still further their relationship, if you could call it that.

He said, 'Have you fixed up about mail? At times up there it's irregular if we can't get across the river and down country to the nearest delivery box, but I suppose you'll want your parents to have an idea of your whereabouts.'

'One of the nurses, Maddie Soames, is going to attend to that,' she told him. 'The mail can still come here. I'll keep in touch with her by phone—I've written to my parents that I'll be travelling round the Alpine region, so if they mark anything urgent, Maddie will open it and phone me. I didn't want them to know access was quite so bad where I was going—simply that I could be here, there, and everywhere as people often are, touring.'

Almost the truth. The fact was she didn't want her

father to know she was going to Thor's Hill, whence
he'd made a sudden departure, evidently leaving no
address. She very much wanted to know why. But this
antagonistic stranger must have no suspicion of that.
He'd think she'd worked George Ramsay's return to
the station for her own ends.

They picked up George, his vivid blue eyes sparkling
with the anticipation of going home to his own place.
His sister, as well as Juliana, had a hotwater bottle to
pack round him, though the car had an excellent
heater. He'd had his medication, Juliana checked the
supplies they were taking, and they waved goodbye to
Matron who had made a point of attending his
departure, and they set off on the main road, running
north a few miles till at Washdyke they would turn west
towards those superb mountains already etched in
snowy brilliance against the blue winter sky, cold and
cloudless.

In deference to Juliana's nursing status, she was in
the back with George, Grizel in front with Tulloch
MacNair. Now and then her eyes met his in the driving
mirror; she felt he was assessing her, looking for
something to criticise, to make her appear to be taking
a risk in making it possible for a sick man to return to
the back of beyond. Yet she didn't want to irk George
with too much fussing.

She said gently, 'I know that with your love of this
country of yours, Mr Ramsay, you'll be dying to point
out all the landmarks, the differences between here and
Scotland, but it's exciting enough, a journey like this,
straight out of hospital, without exhausting yourself
talking. I'm sure Mrs Ramsay and Mr MacNair will
point out a few things, but it ought to be, mainly, a
restful trip. With the night in the Fairlie house, you'll be
refreshed enough to be able to comment on the
undoubtedly more exciting terrain of the last half of the
drive.'

Grizel chuckled in the most sisterly fashion. 'George,
for once you won't be able to give that ready tongue of
yours full rein. I'm going to really enjoy myself. You've
always been able to talk me down. It's mainly rolling

downs, very pastoral, Juliana, till we get nearer the foothills, and beyond Fairlie it changes dramatically. We're very grateful for the Fairlie residence . . . not that it's grand enough to be called that, of course, just an old-fashioned six-roomed house in a side street, but it's a godsend. It enables us to keep married staff at Thor's Hill because it gives the women and children the chance of a few weeks now and then to be able to mix at school, and the mothers to have neighbours to gossip with, plus the novelty of being able to walk along a street to buy a loaf of bread or a joint of meat, to join in local activities, get to church more regularly and so on. Of course when the river behaves we often go to the Church of the Good Shepherd on Lake Tekapo. At present there's just one wife on the station, Barbara Murray, our head shepherd's wife. She loves a break in September or so, even in August if the river's low and they're sick of a white landscape.'

Tulloch MacNair said lightly, 'Watch it, Grizel. At the moment Sister Hendrie is regarding this as a prolonged skiing holiday like she used to take at Kingussie . . . but she might find it palls when you're cooped up with the same people day in, day out, for weeks at a time, with never a blade of grass showing to break the monotony.'

George permitted himself to say, 'Then she must stay on to see our infinite variety when the snows go and the ground thaws and our disease-free flowers come into bloom. No one can appreciate Thor's Hill to the full till they've had the four seasons there.'

Juliana, despite her reservations about the station manager, knew a lift of the heart as mile by mile the chain of magnificent mountains came nearer. It divided the wide East Coast provinces from the narrow bush-clad strip of West Coast that faced the Tasman and far-off Australia. What a watershed it must be. No wonder it had a river called the Rubicon!

Meanwhile these homesteads were charming, with avenues of European oaks, chestnuts, beeches, ashes, rowans, limes, poplars. Some were in such sheltered dips and valleys that a few tattered remnants of autumn's glory still clung to them, others, exposed to the winds sweeping through the passes from the snowy heights, were bare, but showed such an exquisite filigree of black twigs, against the sky, they had a beauty all their own.

Back in the gullies were a few pockets of New Zealand bush—Juliana called it native forest—that were evergreen, impenetrable in spots, eerie, formidable. Perhaps that was why this land bred men like Tulloch MacNair, aloof, enigmatic, austere. The names on the gates became Scots names, some even Gaelic. Grizel said, 'Why that big sigh, Juliana? By the way, I'm not going to call you Sister or Miss Hendrie. I've a daughter older than you.'

Juliana was conscious of colour warming her cheeks and knew Tulloch was watching her in the mirror. Might as well be honest. 'Those names . . . they got to me. *The Cuillins*; *Glen Carron*; *Drumnadrochit* . . . they made me feel homesick for a moment.'

George reached out a gnarled hand and clasped hers, on the rug, 'Don't sound apologetic, lass. We're all that way, or ought to be. Most unnatural if we never, when far away, knew the tug of homesickness, such as I felt so lately, lying in my hospital bed all those weeks. And because of you I can go home—right home. But with regard to you, I hope our peaks and valleys will make up to you a little for your own hills and glens.'

She knew Tulloch must have seen the gesture, and she hoped he wouldn't read too much into it. It was no more than an elderly man's wish to comfort. Pity he was a widower. She'd be afraid to show the natural affection she felt for this gallant veteran of the storm-swept ranges. He reminded her of Grossvater Ruedi.

They came into Fairlie, aptly named, lying sweetly beneath a sheltering half-circle of foothills. It had a last outpost look. Beyond it, she knew, lay Burke's Pass and the famed Mackenzie country, named for a renowned rustler and his dog, lawbreakers but honoured for their daring.

They turned left into a pleasant tree-lined road that could have been one in any of the gentle coastal towns they'd left back east. Juliana imagined that it was a great contrast to the terrain they'd venture into tomorrow, that journey that would end against the impasse of great mountains where the road would dwindle to nothingness in the snow-fed waters of a wild river, beyond which there would be only sheep and cattle and shepherds and a cluster of farm buildings. In front would be that great massif of mountain solidarity, mocking man's endeavours to pass through. The only way to cross the heights was in man-made machines soaring into the sky.

Smoke was curling from a chimney made of glacier stones, planed smooth by billions of years of grinding ice. The sun sparkled from the windows, and as they drove up the curved shingle drive to a stop outside the verandah steps, the door was flung open and a smiling neighbour appeared.

'George, Grizel, Tulloch ... how lovely to see you! And this'll be the Sister Hendrie I heard so much about. George, we'd no idea you were such a fluent letter-writer. Almost lyrical, those letters were. Now take it easy. The house is beautifully warm and I've had the electric blankets switched on since just after breakfast, so there's no chance of unaired beds. The kettle's boiling, and when I've brewed up I'll disappear. You'll want peace and quiet after your journey. Joe will see you tomorrow before you leave. He said of *course* you wanted to be back among your mountains. Nowhere better for convalescence, specially when you could bring you own nurse.'

Juliana was glad to see Mr Ramsay didn't look a whit the worse for his journey. He didn't even sink into his lazy-boy chair in front of the fire. In fact, with difficulty he was persuaded not to do a tour of the garden. Juliana was adamant. 'Mr Ramsay, you won your point about returning to Thor's Hill, but don't push your luck too far. You can see the garden tomorrow. Until you're fully recovered, you're under orders—it's not fair otherwise. I'm responsible for your continuing good health. You're fortunate not to be spending a month in a rest-home!'

George chuckled, reached out an affectionate hand and patted her cheek. 'And it's a charming tyrant you are, lass. I'll give in.'

Juliana would have liked to have wiped that look from Tulloch MacNair's face.

CHAPTER TWO

NEXT morning the real enchantment began, with the road narrowing into Burke's Pass and the first shimmering glance of Mount Cook, towering its twelve thousand three hundred and forty-nine feet behind and above foothills that were great heights in themselves. These were typical of the real tussock country, hills clothed with dry, tufty growth that but for the glitter of the ranges against the sky could have made one doubt this was winter in its desert-like tawniness.

They had an early lunch in a mountain pass where the air was like wine and the sun so hot they had to take care the rolls they were eating with their pannikins of hot soup didn't curl up. Juliana made George have his in the car.

Tulloch joined her at the back of the estate car where she was buttering another roll for her patient. 'Isn't that overdoing it a bit? Insisting he stay inside?' he asked under cover of Grizel's chatter to her brother.

Her eyes met his challengingly. '*I'm* in charge of this patient. Besides, isn't that a thrawn, contrary remark coming from you? I had thought *you* were going to be doing the fussing.'

A matching glint lit his eyes. His voice had a dry note in it—hatefully amused! '*I* think you're being the contrary one. Just to show me, you're going to be over-protective. Poor George!'

The look in her eye now was very much that of the Sister on the ward, complete with starched veil. 'I assure you, Mr MacNair, nothing matters to me except the welfare of my patient. It's so easy to be deceived by this sun. He's better enjoying it behind glass. It would take only a wind to spring up, fresh off those snows, to give him a chill. I'm well aware this is quite a journey for a man newly out of hospital, and I take no chances.

I'm certainly not petty enough to use the situation to score off you.'

She was disconcerted when he laughed. 'One up to you! You're a bonnie fighter, and how surprising. I'd put you down as a human icicle. But watch it, you won't always win.'

Juliana shrugged. 'You're a trifle dramatic, aren't you? You make it sound like a fencing match. I've no interest in crossing swords with you. All I'm keen on is my job. There ... Mr Ramsay is getting his appetite back already. Nothing like the known and familiar to pep up one's spirits.'

Her heart lifted as they sped west, and the mountains became closer. Her own type of country ... and she was looking at terrain her father must have known and loved. If only she could share it with him in a letter! They crested a rise and instinctively Tulloch MacNair drew into the side of the road so they could drink in the sheer beauty of Lake Tekapo spread before them in the shimmering turquoise of its glacial waters. Juliana guessed it wasn't just for her, the newcomer in their midst, but a habit, just as Queen Victoria and Sir Walter Scott had had their own special viewpoints of scenes dearly loved, in Scotland.

Tulloch said slowly, with an emotion in his voice that meant that for him this was the 'one spot beloved over all' Kiplingwise, 'James Maxwell described it best, I think, in his booklet, as a "spread of vivid blue waters cupped in the palm of the Two Thumb Range. The shores, unexpectedly free of buildings, present a scene of almost primeval landscape." It's evidently a combination of the clear water draining into it, intense ultra-violet light, clean air and blue sky. I believe he said that too.'

Juliana said, her own voice husky in tribute, 'Beauty like that almost hurts. Perhaps because there's so much in our world today that's ugly and pitiful and cruel. What have we done to deserve beauty and peace like this?'

George patted her hand again. He said to Grizel, but

she felt it was directed at Tulloch, 'Just the girl for here, isn't she? I believe she'll even take the stark loneliness of Thor's Hill in her stride.'

The village was set back from the lake, thronged with trees, dotted with holiday houses and chalets, with colourful roofs set among gardens that were beautiful even in winter. They called at the modern store for still more provisions, then were away.

They ran along the east side of Lake Tekapo for miles, and by the feel of the road, hard frozen into deeply scored ruts, knew they were getting into alpine regions all right. This road ran on till it finished against another river barrier, the Macaulay, which had to be crossed to get to Lilybank, one of the famous Great Divide stations of the area, but they would turn off slightly east, to pass the access to Craigievar till the road dwindled at their own crossing.

And what a road it became! More of a track. Parts of it Juliana guessed would be impassable with mud after heavy snow and the subsequent thaw, or in times of driving rainstorms. It dipped and swung round shoulders of lesser heights, climbed and skirted great streams that were almost rivers, only one or two roughly bridged. They saw the turn-off to Craigievar, and here were two mailboxes, stuck out in the wilderness.

'They come no farther than this,' said Grizel. 'At times when the river's impassable even with the four-wheel-drive truck, one of the men will ride through, if we deem it safe enough, to leave and collect mail. At Craigievar the river is narrower and deeper and confined to one stream because it's forced through a small gorge higher up. But at Thor's Hill the Rubicon is spread out into a braided river, with about seven streams intersecting the heavy shingle bed. The track through it is well marked with poles.'

'How far from Fairlie is the homestead?'

'Right to the door it's exactly seventy miles. No good quoting you in kilometres, I suppose. We've been metric for a while.'

Juliana ignored that. With her mixed parentage she

was as familiar with one as the other. 'I think George said the acreage was huge, not far off a hundred thousand acres? Then how many sheep do you carry?'

'Seven thousand. Could take far more in summer, but we're only allowed as many as we can winter. And it's more than enough when it comes to snow-raking, even if helicopters have made it more easy.'

It seemed vast enough to Juliana, used to the small Swiss farm of her grandparents. They came to the Rubicon, drove the Holden into one of a row of rough outbuildings that hardly deserved to be called garages, and transferred the gear to the doughty-looking four-wheel-drive Army vehicle Tulloch backed out of another. He picked up a phone, wound the handle and said into it, 'Barbara? We're on our way, see you soon.'

There would have been room for Grizel beside George in the cab of the truck, but she refused it. 'I'm not letting Juliana ride alone through a river, in the back. You'll make me feel old if you insist. After all, think of the perilous drives in the gig in our young days!'

Tulloch MacNair settled them firmly, packing stuff round them, then said, 'Sister Hendrie ... there's one rule. Don't look over the side and look down, it can make you dizzy. The river's low today, but one stream is running a bit swiftly and may be scoured out. The stones shift a bit under us ... don't panic. We're used to it.'

Before they had negotiated half the streams, Juliana was aware that though she'd felt like belittling Mount Cook's size to Tulloch, even knowing it was a respectable height, if not equalling the Eiger or the Gros Glockner, she couldn't despise this river. It was like no other she had ever crossed. The tug of the waters, the seeming inadequacy of the marking poles in a river whose channels could hold the jellyish consistency so fine that it formed quicksands, all added up to fearsomeness.

Grizel didn't speak till the last, deepest stream was crossed and Tulloch, with superb driving skill, headed

the truck on to firmer shingle that actually had the
semblance of tyre tracks and a faint hint of a roadway
leading on.

Tulloch MacNair eased up, stopped, put his head out
of the side and said, 'Well, Sister Hendrie, you've
crossed your Rubicon.'

Indeed she felt she had.

Surprise upon surprise was what Juliana knew as they
breasted the rise from the river. She had expected to see
the homestead before her immediately. Instead a long
boulder-strewn track snaked across the immense valley
floor and disappeared into infinity. There was never a
tree to break the greyness, just huge rocks stranded here
and there, hinting at mighty forces that in times long
past had swirled these down after wrenching them from
those intimidating mountainsides that but for the
vastness of this flat area would have walled them in
with claustrophobic grimness.

Tulloch pulled up to make sure the women were
comfortable enough. She said, 'I thought the homestead
would have been nearer.'

George got out to stretch his legs and savour the
air. 'Seeing it for the first time makes an impact. The
first settlers were extremely wise. Despite the steep
riverbank, they had no known history of this place to
tell them how high the river might rise in thaw or rain,
so they took no chances. They did well because they
managed to build in a spot that gave them the
maximum of sun in the short hours of winter and also
avoided the worst of the devastating winds. The river
winds around a hill, veers north a little, then swings
round east after it cuts through the gorge, well away
from the homestead buildings, the woolshed, cookhouse,
and the most of the grazing. It's not often you see the
valley floor so clear of snow at this time. Actually, that
was what decided me to chance coming home. I
ascertained from Don Murray that it was clear. I'm not
that thrawn, as Sister Hendrie would say, to attempt it
otherwise.'

Tulloch MacNair said, 'You wouldn't have been

allowed to be thrawn. Don't think you got all your own way, George. It was only because of this that I consented. Cunning hound, ringing Don!'

This man certainly was high-handed! Juliana changed the subject by asking the names of the peaks. They told her, all three vying with each other. Tulloch added, 'And even the less dramatic heights have their own apt names . . . Thunderclap Peak, the Witches' Cauldron, Hurricane Point, meanings not to be taken lightly. The Maori River names have their warnings too. The Awatipua . . . the Channel of the Goblin or demon; the Waimihi . . . the River of Regret. There's a lot in a name.

'Of course,' said Juliana agreeably. 'We have them too, like at Loch Katrine, our *Coire an Uruisg* is the Corrie of the Monster and some of our house-names in Gaelic have quite fearsome meanings related to clan feuds and savage warfare of long ago.'

George nodded, 'But our homestead name wasn't chosen because it thunders more right there, even if it is named for the Norse god of thunder. The first settler here came from Norway, so that name needn't intimidate you. For some reason Tulloch seems bent on playing up the natural hazards . . . but you're not the sort of lass to be put off by a name, are you?'

Tulloch was straightening some of the boxes that had skidded round the tray of the truck coming up from the river, but he looked up and met Juliana's eyes. She couldn't resist it, she wrinkled her nose, the gamin look superseding the calm one, and giggled. 'Nothing's more calculated to make me feel at home, Mr MacNair, than the name of the homestead. I kept meaning to tell George. Our small property at home in Scotland is called Ben Thor.'

Well, at least this craggy giant of a man could laugh at himself. He said, 'We do enjoy scaring the daylights out of greenhorns as a rule.'

George said affectionately, 'I knew you were the lass for here, but what a coincidence!'

She could have told him it was no coincidence whatever, that it was just another link in the chain of circumstances that had brought her here. She'd known, when George first said what his home was called, that her father must have named his house in Scotland, when he and Mother married, after this faraway place in the Pacific where his boyhood and young manhood had been spent.

Tulloch said, 'Ben Thor ... Thor's Mountain. Of course there are a lot of Norwegian descendants in Scotland, and even more in Orkney and Shetland. I've just realised, that'll be where your colouring comes from, Sister. You're a real Viking lass.'

She shook her head. 'I haven't a drop of Norse blood in my veins—the fair colouring is from Swiss ancestors on my mother's side.'

He nodded. 'Strange how it can crop out generations later.'

She didn't correct him. It wasn't generations ago; her own mother had been born on the shores of Lake Lucerne. She'd better not be too squashing with this man, though. He'd been so scathing about the heights of the Scottish mountains. He'd feel a fool if he knew the Swiss mountains had been the playground of their family holidays since pre-school days. She'd aroused his antagonism enough as it was. Hers was a small secret mission, important only to herself, to find out why her father never mentioned his early days in any detail. The desire to know possessed her.

They swept round a massive shoulder of rock, and there, on their right, like an oasis in the desert, was the homestead and its sheltering trees. Great plantations of larch and fir and Corsican pine were ranged symmetrically on three sides, a stone wall extended each side of the driveway, which had no gates, just cattle-grids, or cattle-stops as she'd learned to call them here, and all over the enclosed area were dotted trees among the huge glacial rocks that could never be bulldozed out, so were part of the natural landscaping.

The homestead sat upon terraces that were mostly due to the area but improved upon by man, she guessed, and they were covered with ground-hugging alpine plants that gave the garden its only touch of colour at this time, sulphur-yellow, sage-green, silver-white, rust-red, and for contrast, here and there, were clots of frozen snow.

Tulloch sounded a gay tattoo on the horn and instantly the house erupted figures. At least three doors flew open. Juliana hadn't expected children, but only one of the four was a grown-up. The girl was the eldest, about eleven. They shot down a succession of steps and met them halfway up the semi-circular drive. She was surprised when Tulloch pulled in goodnaturedly, let them spill out greetings, then said, 'Now, try to race me up.' They went flying up. He put on a big spurt first, then slowed down to allow them to win. Grizel said to Juliana fondly, 'Barbara will have been here all day making sure the house is warm. We're sure lucky in our head shepherd's wife.'

Tulloch assisted them out of the tray of the truck, Grizel kissed Barbara Murray fondly, the men followed suit, while Juliana took the opportunity to take stock of the other woman on the station. Nothing less than a positively ravishing redhead!

Barbara was made known to her, said, 'I guess the children were too excited to be introduced properly, Sister Hendrie, this is our daughter Marian, the little boy is our Jemmy, and this one is Todd.' Juliana felt a tremor run over her . . . how strange to find a nine-year-old boy here bearing the same name as her father once did.

The warmth of the house met them in waves. They went along a stone-floored porch—ideal, Juliana surmised, for kicking off snow-packed boots when the men reached the haven of home after being out on the hill all day. Sure enough, there was a tiered rack of boots where many pairs could stand upside down to thaw out and air, a huge hollowed-out stone urn with alpine sticks in it; an open door revealed a schoolroom, looking unused, and a storeroom, large, with a fascinating whiff of sugar and apples, spices and carrots. Then they took a step up into a large kitchen where a double-ovened red and cream range purred and rumbled and a huge pot emitted broth-like odours.

They explained to her that it was a diesel-fed stove and was never out as it was drip-fed.

This would be the heart of the house. The vinyl floor was covered with colourful sheepskins, thick in the fleece, and a rag mat in front of the stove looked reasonably new so it must be a tradition to always have a rag mat there. Probably Grizel's work. Juliana knew several homes in her own Scots village that could have matched its design of rose and thistle. She hadn't expected to feel such a sense of homecoming, when knowing that as far as Tulloch MacNair was concerned, she was here only on sufferance.

At the far end glowed an open fire piled with logs. Something made her glance up at the ceiling. 'Forgive me if I'm being naïve, but can that possibly be main power? I was sure it would be a power plant of your own. I mean, away out here, at the back of beyond.'

It was Tulloch who answered, and this time didn't make her seem foolish. 'We like people to be surprised—makes us feel positively metropolitan! You must have missed seeing the pylons. Main power has been here over a score of years. We had it not long after they raised Lake Tekapo. It made all the difference to life up here. I didn't know it in pre-electricity days. My people didn't come here till I'd finished school, but it means so much to the women. Especially for bread— bread-making takes so long. It's also marvellous to be able to store strings of sausages, lashings of venison, and Canada geese and chickens, to say nothing of pies and scones and cakes so we're never sent into a flap with unexpected visitors.'

Juliana shot him a suspicious glance. 'You're having me on! You can't get unexpected visitors here. They have to be brought over the river on the four-wheel-drive.'

'One up to you. Unexpected is merely in a manner of speaking. True, visitors don't just drop in, like in town, but there one always has a corner shop. Here we call 'em unexpected if they ring from the riverbank to say they've been at Lake Tekapo and couldn't resist coming the rest of the way, and could we come and get 'em? It used to be a case of whatever was in the larder, but now there's always something homemade just needing thawing. We get more company than you'd expect.'

Barbara said, 'Before anything else you're to sit down and have a bowl of broth. It'll put warmth into you after that ride.' Juliana was conscious of an echo of Highland hospitality and kinship. This girl looked up to the minute, but it could have been any kindly Scots neighbour saying, 'Come awa' in and have a bite.'

It was delicious cockie-leekie soup, full of vegetables, eaten with crisp rolls warm from being on the stove-rack. Todd heaved a sigh of repletion. 'It's a good idea having a sort of extra meal in between other meals, isn't it? I get awfully hungry about this time. You can have too much routine.'

The tussocky man chuckled. 'I know the feeling . . . like midnight feasts, for instance.'

'Yep,' Todd grinned at his mother. 'Like that terrible time I couldn't get to sleep because of my . . . my . . . what did you call it, Mum? It was a funny feeling in my stomach really, but you said it was my——?'

Barbara's lips twitched. 'Your conscience, son. But it doesn't matter any more. You owned up, so that put paid to it.'

Todd wasn't having any of that. 'Oh, it was more than just a little sort of badness. I'd been *really* wicked. And I . . . um . . . involved other people to boot. My cousins, who were staying here. I'd been *so* bad I didn't think there was any chance of God forgiving me. I knew Mum would, sooner or later, but she eggsplained that that was making God out to be not so kind as *she* was, and however forgiving a mother was, God was even more so. Still, I *do* think it must've taken God all his time to get round to forgiving me. Gosh, I was bad! I——'

Barbara rose, handed him the roll-basket. 'Put what's over in the bread-bin, please. And, son, don't fall into the trap of boasting about your sins—that'd be worse still. We did have a good picnic that night, didn't we?'

They all stared at Barbara, and she giggled. 'Yes, his dad thought me crazy too, but I had to get him back to normal and catch up on sleep myself, so we had a snack.'

Todd got in. 'I'll say! We had bread with cauliflower pickle spread on it, that's my favourite, and cheerio sausages and a strawberry milk shake!'

Tulloch said in a tone of great respect, 'Barbie, you must have a cast-iron digestive system if you could sleep a wink after that in the middle of the night!'

Marian said, 'Can I show Sister Hendrie to her room, Mum? I helped get it ready.'

'You *may*,' said her mother pointedly. Then to Juliana, 'Sorry to sound pedantic, but I take these children for their correspondence lessons, and it makes you that way. Marian, it doesn't mean you can fire dozens of questions at her, or do her unpacking. People like to unpack their own things.' She said, in an aside to Juliana, 'And preserve what privacy is possible here.'

Juliana knew she was going to like Barbara and her heart lifted. No tension here. So pooh to Tulloch of the Tussocks! She said gaily, 'Come on, Marian, you could be a help.'

From the outside the homestead had looked like a house that had been added to by everyone who'd ever lived here, very haphazardly, with no reference to an architectural plan, but happily it had resolved itself inside into a harmonious whole. It straggled all over the place, with odd little steps and passages, that made it seem like a succession of separate wings.

'Mum thought you should have the room next to Uncle George's in case you have to get to him during the night, and Thor's is the other side of his. He did all the night nursing when he first took ill.'

'Thor? Who is——'

'Tulloch,' explained Marian. 'I started it when I was wee. I had a book called *Mar of Mar's Hill*, so I called him Thor of Thor's Hill, and it sort of stuck. Suits him, doesn't it?'

It did too, a mountain man, one with the elements, a man of storms, of thunder, or the wildfire that played round the peaks.

The room was a delight—not exquisitely furnished or

even with a strong colour scheme, but it was so cosy, so welcoming. A bed-sitting-room. It had a deep couch, a couple of shabby wing-backed chairs, a fireplace fashioned out of the local stone, a wall-to-wall carpet in an old-fashioned rose design mellowed by age and the fierce suns of the region into pastel harmony. The bed had a knitted cotton quilt, dyed green to modernise it, a small desk and a chiffonier on which stood a tray with a morning-tea set on it, an electric jug and caddy and biscuit-barrel.

A bookcase, well filled, completed it and on top stood the only floral decoration, if it could be called that, a large spray of dried flax flowers, as black as if carved from ebony, and at the base was a cluster of scarlet berries, the only vivid splash of colour. Marian was watching Juliana's face, so now she clapped her hands. 'You like it, don't you?'

'I love it. How cosy I'll be! I won't need to sit over the family the whole time—that's what I prefer in private cases. Goodness, is that a shower through there? How luxurious!'

'Yes, I'm afraid there's no bath, but there's one along the next passage. This is the next best thing, though. It's a Shrub. That means a shower with a deeper floor and a plug, and you sit down in it and scrub yourself if you need it or want to. That door through there leads into Uncle George's room, but he doesn't look ill enough to need nursing at night, I guess.'

'That's true, Marian, but it's reassuring to a nurse to be able to peep in on her patient now and then. I appreciate that.' Suddenly Juliana wanted to giggle. If Tulloch MacNair was still harbouring the absurd idea that George Ramsay felt in any way amorous towards his nurse, he'd raise those remarkably bushy eyebrows of his at this close proximity!

'You can help me unpack,' she told Marian. 'Everything except the books. Put everything on the bed, then we'll decide which drawers to use.'

Marian said wisely, 'Are they the sort of books not suitable for my age?'

'No, I only meant I shan't want them right away.

This place is overflowing with books, so I shan't be forced to re-read my own favourites. I don't want to spare too much time for this in case Mr Ramsay needs me. I'll want him to have a rest.' That was a good excuse. She didn't want this bright child to see that latest book of her father's, *The Unconquerable Ridge*, and put two and two together. Time enough.

Everything had been well prepared, the pipes from the central heating were pleasantly warm. Mr Ramsay's room gave her a pang for him. Till now she'd not been conscious of the loss of his marriage partner, Grizel had seemed so adequate. But here was a wide sturdy bed, with a hand-quilted spread on it. There were two fireside chairs. This would be where, in pre-central heating days, Polly Ramsay had nursed her babies for their early morning feeds. The fire would never have been allowed to go out in winter. Her photo was on his bedside table, and her darning basket, slung on rails like a baby's bassinet, stood beside it. No doubt she darned his socks here. Odd how a stranger coming in saw only the present-day family, not the ones who'd been its life-blood in other years. She looked up to find Tulloch MacNair surveying her from the doorway.

'Satisfied with your quarters?' he asked coolly.

Juliana's tone was equally cool. 'Perfectly, thank you. Couldn't be better. I like the largeness of the rooms, the close proximity to my patient. He still needs some attention at night.'

'My room is the other side of his, not connected, but handy enough. I'll leave my door ajar. Don't hesitate to call me.'

'I hope I shan't have to,' said Juliana. 'After all, I'm here to save the family just that.'

The look he bent upon her seemed almost accusing. 'Sister Hendrie, I hope that because I wasn't pleased about Mr Ramsay coming up here straight from hospital, you aren't going to be petty and refuse to allow me to help when it might need two.'

There was a hint of contempt in the green eyes. 'Mr MacNair, that would be entirely unprofessional. It would mean I was risking my patient's welfare in order to stress to you that I'm capable of managing on my own. However, if Mr Ramsay continues to improve as he's doing, I probably won't need any help with him.'

She expected some comeback, a whiplash retort, but deflatingly he disappointed her. 'Good . . . as long as I know you aren't too stiff-rumped to ask for help. George's welfare is all I care about. I wanted him back here, to satisfy his longing for home, but only if he was well enough to take it. I wanted no last crossing of the Rubicon for him yet.'

For the first time a tremor of fear ran over Juliana. He looked at her sharply as she controlled the shiver. Then he said quite gently, which disarmed her, 'Sorry, that was a bit rough on you. He's far stronger than I thought he'd be after all those weeks in hospital. But you know how it is with one's nearest and dearest.'

Her eyes searched his. 'Your nearest and dearest?'

He nodded. 'Grizel and George are my only relatives, plus their children. They're all away, or married, and never likely to live here permanently again. George refers to me as his nephew, but I'm really a younger cousin, several times removed. He had daughters, no sons, and rightly, when they married, those daughters followed their men. One of them, like Grizel did, married a minister of religion, the other is building roads in Papua. So there was only me to carry on. It pleases George to call me his nephew.'

She got the picture. His nephew and heir. So to all intents Tulloch MacNair *was* the master of this property, all one hundred thousand acres. In very truth, Thor of Thor's Hill. His was the say-so. She must walk warily. Well, possibly she needed only a month in which to find out why her father, an outgoing man in all else, was so reticent about his early life here. George's comment niggled at her with increasing uneasiness. He'd said Polly, his wife, had always yearned after young Todd, had hoped he wouldn't go to the bad. Why? Surely he hadn't shown signs that he might? Had there been a potentiality for wrongdoing? Not *Dad*! Oh, no, *not* Dad.

She said crisply, 'I've satisfied myself his room is

ready and well aired, so soon as I note signs of
weariness I can get him to bed. I was tempted to suggest
he have dinner in bed, but I feel it would frustrate him.
One of the joys of convalescence is feeling oneself back
in the family circle again. It would be a good idea, Mr
MacNair, if after the meal, while we're washing up,
you came in here with him. It's very comfortable, and
no doubt he'll be eager for details of the station work.
That could keep his interest up while not involving him
in manual effort. Yes, that's an idea.'

The brows twitched, the derisive note tinged his
voice. 'I can see we're all going to dance to your piping.'

Juliana sighed. 'A moment ago you spoke of him
being your nearest and dearest. It would be a small
thing to expect of you when you can't possibly work
outside. Convalescents need family and company as
much as tablets and nursing.'

She heard the whiplash then. 'My dear girl, it was
meant to be a joke. I even think it's a good idea. I do
hope you've some sense of humour.'

She lifted her chin. 'That's always an offensive
remark, having one's sense of humour doubted. None
of our dealings so far, Mr MacNair, have led me to
believe you have even a gleam of humour in your make-
up.'

She could have stamped her foot when he laughed. 'I
begin to have hopes of you—you've actually got a
temper! As I said, I'd put you down as a human icicle,
all starch and white veils, saying the most calm and
unshakable things in that laying-down-the-law tone that
seems to come with passing medical exams. But if
you've got a paddy, it'll do Thor's Hill. We get enough
snow and ice. And by the way, don't get into uniforms,
will you? Slacks and sweaters are the rule up here. Sheer
necessity.'

This time Juliana allowed herself a twinkle. 'Did you
say *I* laid down the law? It's up to me what I wear. I do
know enough to come in out of the cold! But the only
time I'll don uniform is if Mr Ramsay disobeys me as I
gradually relax supervision, and gives himself a setback.
Then I'll put a uniform on over my sweater and treat

him like an invalid. Now, I must get back to my patient and perhaps help Mrs Ramsay with the finishing touches of the dinner.'

'You mentioned doing dishes before,' he remarked. 'You don't have to, you know. You're simply engaged to look after George. We don't expect you to pitch in with the housework.' He added, 'I'm trying to remember that if you took private cases in Scotland or England, it could be quite different. So much more domestic help over there.'

'Not now, or not as much. You get it in the very big houses. I've no intention of allowing Mrs Ramsay to wait upon me—she's older than my own mother.'

'Fair enough. As long as you realise it's not expected or taken for granted. And take a few hours to yourself now and then to compensate for days off being impossible here half the time.'

They had their dinner early for George's sake, though he was very relaxed and happy. It was a pleasant meal, a casserole of venison, fresh vegetables from Fairlie, rings of onion delicately browned, and jacket potatoes encased in foil ready to be split and topped with butter. 'We've even got parsley,' said Grizel happily, 'I brought some from the Fairlie garden. And we've the luxury of fresh cream. We don't keep cows now, Juliana. The cowhands never stayed long, were more trouble than they were worth, and milk and cream had to be scalded every day, so when we've not been out to Tekapo township for some time, we use dried milk. I hope you don't dislike it. Though you get used to it.'

'I like dried milk, I've had it a lot,' Juliana assured her.

'Have you?' Tulloch's voice was surprised. 'I didn't think you'd ever have been on anything but town supply.'

She didn't want to say it was on expeditions with her father. No, she must feel her way carefully before there were any revelations. She said carelessly, 'Oh, Dad used to take us rock-climbing around the Highlands and the Lake District, so dried milk it had to be.'

They probably thought of that Lake District as Cumberland and Westmorland, and had no idea she meant the Swiss Lakes and the high tops. Good. It was almost fun.

She had cleared the table and was pushing it back over the long form against the wall that was used, they'd told her, if the cook was away and the men had to eat up here. She glanced at the wall above it and caught in her breath. There was her father's poem written when he'd been so young. It was beautifully framed. How small Todd Powers must have appreciated the loving thought Polly and George had given to it. A rectangular frame, with the poem about a summer July one side, and the winter July the other.

It was done in Gothic lettering in black, with the capitals wreathed about with intricate whorls and flowers. Even then her father must have been quite good at that. It was a hobby with him now.

George noticed her interest and said, 'That's the poem I told you of, Juliana. Take your time to read them both. No hurry for the dishes. He did that printing at the very table you're leaning on.'

So she stood there, her back to them, and read the lines she knew by heart, because she had to have time to blink the tears back, the tears that had welled up when she'd seen that signature ... Todd Powers. Had he really wanted to sign it Fergus T. Hendrie, his own name?

The moment held magic. Here she was, among the mountains that had inspired that poem, and Mother and Dad were among even taller peaks, in the Himalayas. The words wavered and danced before her eyes ...

'. . . July with her sunsets aflame on the snows,
July with her dawnings of coral and rose,
July with her rainbows that straddle the mountains . . .'

Incredible as it seemed, that world awaited her outside. The rainbows, the sunsets, the dawnings. She mustn't use her handkerchief or wipe the tears away with her fingers, to attract notice ... she blinked rapidly, conquered them, turned back and picked up their pie-plates, which gave her the opportunity to look down.

George asked if he could stay up till the washing-up was done, and have coffee with them. They were all happy about this.

Juliana decided she just loved Grizel. She said to her, 'Thank you for asking me to call you Grizel ... it's a name I'm familiar with. It means, among other things, doesn't it?—Stone-heroine. How fitting for here. The heroine of the rocks, of glacier stones.'

Grizel, whipping plates through the soapy water with rapidity, nodded. 'Mother was keen on meanings and I was born up here, among the crags.' She laughed, 'Well, not literally, in fact in the room that became George and Polly's. George was born at Fairlie. I was in a hurry to get into the world. Mother was thrilled, she used to say, because it didn't mean spending weeks away, waiting for the baby, because they always got the women out in heaps of time in case the river rose. Sometimes it was just as hard to get back. We didn't have such good transport then, just drays, or horseback.

'But it scared the hell out of my father when he got back from one of the huts to hear a newborn baby crying. She hadn't been alone, a shepherd's wife who'd assisted at births before was with her.' She added, 'There, that's the last. I'll make the coffee now and you can get George off. Thor's going to sit with him for an hour or so and you're going to relax with a book or something.'

Juliana knew what she was going to do, but a little later. She couldn't bear to go to bed this night and not go out to keep a tryst with the stars and the mountains ... and her parents. She would feel so close to them.

George, pleasantly tired and immensely content to be home, was resting against a criss-crossed nest of pillows, a detective novel within reach and some wool samples beside him, and was muttering things like fibre diameter and staple-length and colour and crimp, which

was double Dutch to Juliana but seemed to afford him
great satisfaction. Tulloch had lit a small fire in the
bedroom despite the hot pipes, because the old fellow
liked it, reminding him of the pre-electricity days when
he and Polly had so often lain in that self-same bed and
watched the flickering flames.

George looked up with an appeal in his eyes as
Tulloch came in. 'I'd like to go over these with you, lad,
if you can be bothered.'

Tulloch's tawny eyes glinted with mock servility.
'Only if Sister Hendrie there will permit it. You're
supposed to be relaxing.'

Her own eyes glinted back and a dimple cleft her left
cheek. 'I trust you, Tulloch MacNair. You appear to
have conceded by now that I'm in charge of the patient,
with or without the uniform or the starch.'

George Ramsay chuckled delightedly. 'This is the
way it ought to be, the give and take of family life, the
teasing and backchat. You'll do here, Juliana Hendrie.
Now off with you to get a bit of relaxation of your
own, and leave me to my manager and nephew.'

She pulled her gamin face at him and went out to the
kitchen. It was good to flop in front of the blazing logs
and dip into a book on local climbs she chose from the
bookcase. She found she was getting drowsy, looked up
at the clock and said to Grizel, 'I'm going outside for a
long look at the night sky. It's so marvellous to be at
close quarters with the mountains again. I'll wrap up
well.'

Grizel looked a little anxious. 'This is terrifying
terrain, very different from your surroundings in
Scotland, I imagine. Don't go off the terraces, and put
the lights on behind the ranch-sliders. You mustn't be
tempted to take the track. Side-tracks go off it, with
burns crossing them. No street lights . . . and no moon
tonight.'

It made sense. Juliana nodded. 'I'll go down the
terraces and up the side-drive. I promise not to stray.'

She muffled herself up in a brown sheepskin-lined
coat, pulled a scarlet ski-cap with a jelly-bag top and
tassel to it over her ears, wound a big green muffler

round her throat and thrust her hands into wool-lined mitts. All doubts and ruffled sensibilities left her as she stepped into the world she knew and loved . . . of starlit mountains, fleecy clouds, piercing cold and exhilarating tanginess, all silver and pure, with the light that was unearthly.

CHAPTER THREE

JULIANA let the silence seep into her soul. There was a radiance and glory about it that swept all tensions away. The jagged contours were outlined against a sky of blue velvet shimmering with a myriad worlds, each vast in itself yet from here as small as sequins. She was glad there was no moon; when the moon was absent, one felt nearer the stars. She stood at the foot of the centre terrace steps. It was light enough to distinguish the hands on her watch. She was waiting for half-past eight. Just a few minutes to go.

The minute hand moved to the exact position. In that moment she was linked to her mother and father. It was as if they clasped hands about the globe and set distance at naught. In New Zealand, where the sun first touched the earth, she was to think of them at this time. In India it would be two in the afternoon. In Scotland, her brother and sister would be thinking of them in the beauty of a summer morning. She lifted a hand in gay salute, waved it at the distant mountains and said in a whisper, 'Goodnight, my darlings.'

When a voice shattered the silence she jumped, then turned. Tulloch MacNair. He apologised, 'I saw you wave and thought you must have seen me, though you appeared to be waving at the mountains.'

She said slowly, 'We have a pact in our family, because we've been separated so often. We think of each other at a given time every twenty-four hours. Liesel and Robert know what time it is in New Zealand and Mother and Father work out wherever they are on their travels, for both of us.' She wouldn't mention the Himalayas.

'So you were saluting them. It will seem to bring them nearer.'

'It does. It goes back years. Dad's job took him away a great deal, though it's not so bad now Mother's free

45

to go with him. It cropped up once when we were
young. Dad told us to remember that even if we were in
different hemispheres, we were only distant from each
other by the span of time from a sunset to a sunrise.
That the sunset that was closing our day was waking
him up at the bottom of the world.'

'Was he in Australia or New Zealand?'

'No, South America. Chile.' (He'd been climbing in
the Andes.)

He said, 'I was alarmed when Grizel said you'd gone
outside to see the night sky over the Alps, but she told
me you'd promised to go no further than here, and
leave the lights on up above.'

'I know it would be foolhardy to venture further, that
it could involve other people in danger, searching. This
isn't territory to be taken lightly. It will have a history
of risks taken and lives almost lost because of it, I
suppose.'

She thought his voice had a controlled steadiness as
he answered. 'Not just *almost* lost. Mountains and
river have taken quite a toll of lives.'

Juliana knew an appalled moment. He'd said George
was his next of kin. Had his parents——?

She said, 'I hope I've not blundered. That the river
hasn't meant bereavement close to you?'

Tulloch shook his head. 'You mean my parents? No,
thank God I don't have to associate their loss with the
Rubicon or these ranges. They lost their lives in a city
street, after all the years of survival here. A getaway car
after a bank robbery mounted the footpath where they
were strolling. Incredible it should have happened to
them.'

'Mr MacNair, I'm sorry. I do hope you weren't just
a boy?'

'No, I was twenty-three. But we'd been great pals.
George and Polly were magnificent.' He paused,
added, 'We brought them back here to our own
burial ground—it was necessary to have one in the
old days.'

Unthinkingly she said, 'I like the idea of that. My
father has always said——' She stopped abruptly.

He glanced at her, then prompted, 'Your father has always said . . .?'

She had to finish it. It needn't give anything away. 'He's always said he'd like to be buried among mountains.'

'I can understand that, living in the Highlands.'

He added, 'We've got on to a sombre note, for your first night at the back of beyond. Grizel would take me to task. Most of the deaths from drowning were back in time, when men, sick of the solitude, risked a flooded river to get away from it or disobeyed orders. Some were heroic deaths, trying to save others. But none of it need worry you. You're having a working holiday. We'll see it isn't attended with any danger. On those things my ruling is absolute. No one leaves the station unless I okay it. When you're safely in Scotland again, with roads going past your door, you'll remember only the beauty of this.'

He seemed to be emphasising that she was on a visiting status only. One of many, no doubt, who'd come to the station for two or three weeks and departed, leaving hardly a ripple. A strange feeling hit her. Why did she suddenly feel resentful that she wouldn't see the four seasons come to this mountain valley? It must be because her father had spent part of his boyhood here, and later, part of his youth. Dad had almost seemed rootless, not like Mother who could go back any time to her own village on the banks of Lake Lucerne. Here, somewhere, lay the key to the reason for her father's reticence. She turned, said, 'We must go in.'

Morning brought an even greater impact of beauty, because it was one of dazzling winter sunshine that made an unbelievable backdrop of cobalt blue sky, crystal-sharp peaks and glimpses of retreated glaciers with ice-blue clefts here and there. It was a terrific contrast to the broad valley beneath intersected by stream-beds where from the immense gashes in the contours the waters forced their way through to plough their channels in the shingly terrain. Everywhere sheep grazed among the tawny tussocks and snow-grass.

Tulloch MacNair permitted George—there was no other word for it but permitted—to take his nurse to inspect the other buildings on the estate, beautifully and strategically placed for sun and shelter. Tulloch accompanied them, to Juliana's dismay. He was evidently checking that George didn't overtire himself.

'We won't go near the married couple's house,' he told them. 'Barbara has the children in their schoolroom from half-past seven till twelve, except for playtime, then from one till two. Early start, but it ensures they get some afternoon sunshine, essential in winter when we lose the sun so quickly. She was a teacher when she was single, so it's not as tough on her as on some wives. Some interruptions are inevitable, but we don't make them unnecessarily.'

The men's quarters were good, quite new-looking, with a small cookhouse leading off one side. George had pointed out to Juliana the shearers' quarters and big old cookhouse as they came. 'In the old days that sufficed, but as times improved better facilities were indicated. You get all sorts among the permanent hands, some good mixers, some liking their privacy, so we made each room a sort of bedsitter with a couple of easy chairs, their own electric kettle and toaster, bookshelf and radio. We've not got television yet, though it's coming. Costs a fortune, of course. The next property to us, Craigievar, has it, but they're better placed for reception. We're a bit hemmed in. However, we're working on it for next season. It'd make it easier to get an extra couple, especially with children. It may be a mixed blessing, TV, but so many programmes are educational, it helps children with current affairs. Of course the Murray children have never been used to it except at Fairlie during the holidays.'

Juliana looked up at George. 'Have they been here as long as that?'

'Yes, they came up when Marian was a year old. Todd was born here—well, at Fairlie. We regard him as belonging to Thor's Hill.'

'Todd was born here? Then——' she cut off, but

Thor's next words gave her the answer to the question she'd better not ask.

'Barbara so identified herself with this station that because she loved that poem Todd Powers wrote, she called her own son Todd and said she hoped he became as fond of the mountains as that poem expressed.'

Warmth flooded Juliana's heart. That was something she just might be able to tell her father some day ... that he was remembered in a very real way here, no matter why or how he had left it.

They came into the cookhouse where an elderly man was bending over a glowing wood-range. Tulloch was carrying a heavy bag of strings of sausages and saveloys frozen hard, that they'd stored overnight but were destined for the deep-freeze here. He went to sling them on a small table near the door, but the man dropped his ladle back in his soup-pot and said hurriedly, 'Dinna put it there. That table's too femma.'

Tulloch stopped in his action, said bewilderedly, 'Femma? What on earth do you mean?'

Juliana burst out laughing. 'He means it's rocky, fragile ... oh, Mr Willocks, you must be from Tyneside.'

A broad grin spread over Willock's face. 'Aye, that I am, hinny. Are you a Geordie too?'

She grinned, 'I wish I could say: "Why aye, man," but I've got to confess I'm further north—the Highlands. But I nursed for a short spell in Newcastle. I thought femma the most expressive word. And marra.'

Tulloch and George stared. 'You've lost us,' said George. 'It's a foreign language. What's marra?'

'One's workmate. Or more correctly, I suppose, one's mate down the pit.'

'Well, we're learning something from the greenhorn in our midst,' said Tulloch.

Willocks said to Juliana, 'Mebbe you'd not be above coming ower some time for a crack about Newcastle. It's forty years since I've been there and they tell me I wouldna recognise the skyline now, from the bridge.'

'No, possibly not. Like the London one, from Tower Bridge, the skyscrapers and concrete jungles are

usurping the old familiar landmarks of the long-ago
photos, though I can't remember it any other way.
Nevertheless, there are some of the old buildings, very
lovely ones, preserved in Newcastle,' she told him.

They didn't delay, Willocks had three hungry men
coming in at noon, and his midday dinner needed the
last touches. The homestead kept different hours in the
main, having their big meal at night. Juliana said, 'In
any case, George should bé back now for a light lunch
and a rest.'

Willocks grinned. 'It's something to see the old boss
under orders from a bonnie lass like this one! Time was
when he'd ha' paid no heed.'

George laughed. 'Aye, that's true, but even an old
codger like myself can succumb to that bonnie lass. A
lot depends upon who's giving the orders. Right, we'll
let this fetching tyrant have her way.'

Juliana noticed Tulloch didn't join in with the
laughter. Surely he wasn't still harbouring the thought of
a nurse and a susceptible widower? She felt her temper
rise and subdued it. It was too ridiculous. On the heels
of that came the unwelcome thought that these things
did happen. Pity. It made all one's attentions suspect
and poisoned what could have been a delightful
interlude in New Zealand's Southern Alps.

To the devil with Thor of Thor's Hill and his
thunderclap of a descending brow! She would not let
him affect her so that she was starchy and distant with
dear old George. He deserved the very best professional
attention, plus that indefinable warmth that would
make him feel not a liability but a character to whom it
was a privilege to minister.

By the end of a week that by comparison with early
records was the mildest ever known, Juliana felt she'd
been here half a lifetime. The routine of the days had
lulled her into a feeling that time itself could reveal to
her just why her father had been so cagey about his
early life. They had loved the little boy Todd here, had
been flattered and glad that he had returned as a youth,
and had even yearned after him whatever the

circumstances of his sudden departure. That much she
had gathered. She hadn't dare display too much
curiosity.

Strange how growing familiarity dulled the edges of
things. She was becoming used to the rough-hewn facets
of Tulloch's character. Or should she call them rough-
hewn? Weren't they rather an assumption of authority
that sat very naturally on his broad shoulders? She had
met it before, in her own place. Yes, that was who he
reminded her of . . . one of the lairds. George was very
much the 'old boss' the retired high-country farmer
handing over the reins to his heir, an heir who had
proved himself worthy of the position for years.

George talked a lot about his nephew. 'Losing his
parents like that aged him five years. He took on all his
father's responsibilities here—gave up a trip to the
Himalayas he'd been promised. He's got the makings of
a first-class mountaineer, you know, and he had the
chance of joining a New Zealand expedition, in a
humble sort of capacity. It would have realised a dream
for him. But he didn't hesitate. More for my sake and
Polly's than his own. It was when Polly's illness first
showed up, and he knew I'd want to be away from the
station from time to time when she was in hospital. It
was heart, so she had to be in Auckland for surgery.
But they made a grand job of it and spared her to me
for years, so I could come back here. I could rest more
easily knowing Thor was at the helm.'

'Oh, you sometimes call him Thor too?'

'Yes, I've slipped into the habit. That was young
Marian's doing. He'll certainly be Thor of Thor's Hill
in time, and it suits him.'

That sounded like a compliment, from George.
Juliana had at first dubbed him as Tulloch of the
Tussocks. Now she thought of him as Thor. He was,
more aptly, a man of thunder. An unexpected thought
struck her. Her father would have liked Tulloch
MacNair. If he'd gone with that expedition to the
Himalayas, the two men might have met. She shrugged
the thought away. She didn't want to admire the man.
He hadn't wanted her here, and for sure he'd do his

best to get her back over the Rubicon once George no longer needed her. So she'd better not forget that her primary concern was to find why Todd Powers had left this station, never to return; not only that, but never to even name it to his family. He wasn't a reticent man, he was open, loving, an extrovert in all things, save this.

At lunchtime Tulloch looked across at Juliana and said, 'You knew you were having company tonight, didn't you?'

Her eyes widened. '*I'm* having company? What do you mean? How can I, up here?'

'You're insulting my men. Never do to let them think they're not considered company. They told me this morning—said they were coming up to play Scrabble. I've never heard anything like it. I don't reckon they've ever played before. It's wonderful what a bit of feminine company will do. Especially a Scandinavian blonde . . . sorry, a Swiss blonde. I knew this'd happen.'

Juliana recovered from her astonishment. 'Don't be stupid! That was a joke. I was having a yarn with Willocks and the boys wanted to know if they could come up for a game of cards. I told them I was so dumb I couldn't tell one card from another, that even my father said he could have a better game with a chimpanzee than with me and I said if they wanted parlour games I'd give them a go at Ludo or Scrabble any night! I was putting them off.'

'It'd take more than that. You're the only unattached female this side of the Rubicon. They're coming, anyway. Not Willocks.' He looked straightly at Juliana. 'He said he'd rather have you to himself any time.'

She made her gamin face at him. 'You know very well it's only to yap about the Tyneside. I'm amazed— he knows every bit of Border history concerning Northumberland and north of it, you could imagine. It fascinates me. Not that I've known much before. We were in the Highlands, but I'm stuffed with knowledge now, in two afternoons.'

Later she followed Tulloch into his office. 'I'm sorry about this,' she said. 'I'm sure all of you at the homestead value your privacy. I thought by saying I'm the world's worst duffer at cards, I'd have spared you that.'

He looked up from his desk. 'You've got the wrong idea. They're often up here—they need to be, for a change of company. They've not been since you came because they thought it might be too much for George. They can be pretty high-spirited and noisy, you know, and——'

He stopped, and Juliana finished it for him. 'Don't bother to have second thoughts. You were going to say that for another thing you don't want to encourage them about me. You need have no fears, I'm not setting my cap at any of them. Hardly!'

He lifted his head to look at her and the glint in his eye was definitely an angry one. 'How snobbish can you get? You mean they're hardly your type? Let me tell you they're the salt of the earth! We don't often get trash up here. The mountains sort men out. Two of them are aiming to go to Lincoln College after this practical experience, and when they can afford it. Collard would go too, but he's got a widowed and delicate mother and helps support his sisters. They might turn you inside out at Scrabble after all. They're damned fine readers.'

She took a step back from the desk the better to glare at him. '*You* were the one who said they'd probably never played Scrabble in their lives, not me! And in any case, you hardly need a degree in English to play it. You've got this fixed idea that a single woman on the station spells trouble. Well, perhaps you've had experience of that, but I'll prove to you it doesn't always happen. You're about ninety years behind the times, and autocratic to boot, Thor of Thor's Hill! You're still mentally in the era that thought all women wanted husbands. First you thought I could be thinking of George as an elderly wealthy widower, owner of a vast high-country station, positively oozing wealth ... and I didn't even know he *was* a widower. I thought Grizel was his wife. Then you warned me not to play merry hell with your men, making me feel like Mata Hari and a film star rolled into one ... look, for years

I've worked in a world where we think more of careers than of men! Gone are the days when getting a husband was every woman's goal. Those were the days of Jane Austen. I have other goals, believe me. There isn't a man here who could make my heartbeat quicken for a single second, for whom I'd want to give up my career.

'I'm an outdoor type, always have been. I lived all my life among mountains except for my training, so I'm relishing this experience after London and Newcastle. You may have warned me not to cause havoc with your presumably woman-hungry men up here ... let *me* warn *you* ... you're to leave me alone to enjoy my own peaceful existence. I'm not looking for any romantic interludes to give a fillip to living in isolation. *My* pulses don't stir easily. Do I make myself clear?'

She turned to sweep out of the office, aware it was a good exit line. Tulloch's chair scraped back. She was tall enough herself, but he towered over her. His hands shot out and grasped her wrists in a grip that bruised. 'Very clear, Sister Hendrie. Except that the lady doth protest too much. I don't believe a word of it!'

Red rags of rage flew in her cheeks. 'You mean you have the nerve to think I *want* to dally with your men? Oh, you—you——'

His laugh could have been heard in the kitchen. 'Not that. I'll believe you there. I mean that ridiculous bit about your pulses not stirring easily. The only way to make me believe that is to prove it.'

She glanced up at him wide-eyed, not taking his meaning for one very fleeting second. Then, as she divined his purpose, she stiffened and turned to flee, but she was too late. She was crushed into his arms, held against him and kissed. Unforgivably he laughed as he brought his mouth down on hers.

In all her life Juliana had never known so swift a change of emotions, and it caught her unawares. One moment she was full of fury, the next she had no breath to maintain that. The first pressure of his mouth had been hard, victorious, then it gentled, and with that gentling there came a singing in her veins such as she had never expected. It was treacherous, undermining

that sustaining anger. Not even in the attraction
Marcus had for her had she felt *quite like this*. With
that realisation she steadied. She willed herself to go
limp, unresisting. Tulloch loosened his grip, but
retained hold of her, as if he thought she might fall.
One hand slipped to her elbow, the other to the nape of
her neck.

She had lost all her colour; the intensity of her
feelings had ebbed it from her. She lifted her chin
spunkily in an endeavour to give him as icy a look as
she could summon, and was disconcerted to find those
long tawny eyes dancing with merriment.

'Liar!' he said. 'Your pulse was positively racing. Just
as mine was. And I guarantee your heart is thudding.'
His eyes dropped to the curves outlined by her green
lambswool sweater.

She said through her teeth, 'I'm not pulsing, I'm
panting . . . with anger. How——'

He held up a hand, 'Now don't be corny. Don't say:
"How dare you!" Career women don't, you know. They
can control any situation. It's too theatrical. Besides, I
still wouldn't believe you. I reckon you learned more
about yourself a moment ago than in all your career
years, my dear Sister.'

She had taken several deep breaths to steady herself
and managed in a cool tone with a hint of amusement
in it, to say: 'Oh come, Tulloch MacNair, you flatter
yourself. I'm twenty-five, not sweet seventeen never
been kissed. You can't imagine that.'

'Of course not, Juliana Hendrie. But that wasn't what
I meant and you know it. I was referring to your
response.'

She was proud of her unwavering tone. 'Again I find
you vain. What can you know of my life before I came
here? Twelve months ago I was engaged . . . or as near
as made no difference. I can only think you're the kind
of man who fancies himself as bringing an iceberg of a
woman to life. I've no use for that sort of arrogance.'

He ought to have been insulted and it infuriated her
that he wasn't. He even laughed. 'You're a gallant
fighter . . . and a good trier, Queen Juliana.' He added,

'What happened? Why didn't you marry him? And don't tell me it's none of my business. I know it isn't, but I'd like to know.'

'Healthy curiosity? Or just prying?'

'Healthy curiosity.'

'His way of life didn't suit me.'

She had the satisfaction of at last seeing him startled. 'Good God! Perhaps you *are* an iceberg after all. Don't women follow their men any more?'

'That wasn't it. There's got to be more in marriage than just attraction. I wanted a marriage like my parents', based on mutual interests as well as love. So that when the fires died down they'd still have a common bond.'

Suddenly the hostility between them seemed to fizzle out.

Tulloch said, waving a hand, 'I was enjoying this set-to, and now, dammit, I find myself agreeing with you. Tell me, *have* those fires died down?'

'You mean, between my parents? No, the fires haven't died down. Mother and Dad have known many separations in their lives but when they meet again, they also have this tremendous friendship.' She paused, thinking of it, then her eyes lit up, 'And they still, somehow, meet as lovers. Children don't usually think those things about their parents, but we three have always been conscious of it.'

He nodded. 'Then you were wise not to settle for less. Sorry I was scathing.'

Another sensation took over Juliana's being. She could *almost* like this man. 'All right—you couldn't know. Any more than I know the things that have shaped *your* life and made you what you are.'

Again a flicker of homour lit his eyes, 'Like vain and overbearing and arrogant.'

She found herself smiling back. Tulloch added, 'Like finding myself making rash statements, judging you for making what was probably a very sensible decision. I've probed into *your* life; will you find it excusable if I tell you I spoke like that because the woman *I* wanted to marry couldn't take *my* kind of life? Perhaps it went deeper with me than I thought and I lashed out.'

Suddenly they heard Grizel's steps at the far end of the lengthy passage. The craggy features of Thor and Thor's Hill crinkled into real humour. 'How are you going to explain your hair coming down?'

It brought back fleetingly the feel of his hand at the nape of her neck. Her left hand went to twist it up into its pleat, but there wasn't time, and the pins were gone. Her eye fell on the Government red tape he had untied from some papers; she scooped it up, swiftly tied back the pale golden strands of hair.

Grizel, as usual, began talking before she got to the door, 'Tulloch, has Juliana started your letters yet? Because I've found another one of mine I'd like her to do before the mail must go. But if she's on yours, perhaps she could cram it in after . . .' the door swung open and she bustled in. 'Oh, she hasn't begun, I see. What a good thing.'

Tulloch said smoothly, 'No, I delayed her. I thought a few things needed explaining.'

'Yes, of course. The terms will be new to her. Juliana, I hope you don't think we're imposing, but when I saw how beautifully you typed my business letters, I couldn't resist telling Thor I was sure you'd not mind doing his. George and I are sorting out slides today so we can show you the whole cycle of the year's farming here, so you'll know he's all right. Oh, you've got your hair down your back in a ponytail. You look ten years younger. It's nice, isn't it, Thor?'

He surveyed Juliana. 'Nice, yes, but I wouldn't say ten years, just about five. That'd make her twenty. Who wants a girl to be just fifteen?'

Grizel gave him a peculiar look, turned and said, 'Well, I'll leave you to it.'

Juliana frowned, 'I'm doing your letters, am I? And I wasn't even asked!'

'Oh, Grizel's an organising soul; comes of being a minister's wife for forty years. I must confess I hate typing. How come you're a touch-typist? Or so she says.'

'Dad made us all take a course in it,' said Juliana. 'Cunning hound . . . that meant whoever was home he

got out of typing his own ...' she stumbled, caught
back the word 'books' and said, 'his own letters. He
had a vast business mail.' Phew!

'Does he still travel a lot? What's he in, oil, or
shipping or something?' asked Tulloch.

She wasn't ready yet to tell him her father was Fergus
Hendrie, once known as Todd Powers. She said
nonchalantly, 'Well, travel, sort of. Conducts tours and
that sort of thing.'

Fortunately his phone rang. She recovered her
composure. His voice warmed, said, 'Oh, Rebecca—yes,
he's fine. The old boy, as usual, fell on his feet. He was
nursed by a most efficient sister from Scotland. She's
having a working holiday in New Zealand. She was
going on to Mount Cook, so the wily old beggar
persuaded her it would save her overseas funds if she
had her holiday here. She rules him with a rod of iron—
a real martinet. He's not allowed to overdo, but neither
is he so restricted he kicks over the traces.'

This Rebecca's voice came over the wire clearly.
'How old is this martinet? In the forties bracket?'

He chuckled maddeningly, 'What are you imagining?
A utility packet, all starch and no nonsense? She's
about your age, my dear Rebecca, possibly a little
younger. A blonde with green eyes ... old George
always had an eye for a good-looker. She has Swiss
ancestors way back, and looks it. She's done skiing in
Scotland and rock-climbing in the Lake District.'

Juliana missed Rebecca's reply because it sounded
through laughter. Tulloch answered, 'Well, I wouldn't
put it past George to have had that in mind. She
certainly has all the qualifications *and* the vital statistics
... wouldn't surprise me if he did have matchmaking in
mind.'

Juliana gave a gasp of protest. It must have carried,
because Rebecca said, 'What was that? It sounded——'

Tulloch guffawed. 'That was Sister Hendrie. She was
right beside me. No, you haven't dropped a clanger. I
could have shut you up, darling Rebecca, but couldn't
resist teasing her. She hasn't got your good opinion of
me—can't think why. We've just had a clanging row.

According to her I'm antiquated ... I've never heard of career women, living up here at the back of beyond ... she doesn't care for my type, I'm overbearing, chauvinistic, vain ... oh, there's no end to what she's called me! She has a fine vocabulary. I wish you could see her face, Rebecca. You'd better come over and assure her that when I'm not been thwarted by a demon of a career woman, I've a lovely nature. What? You *are* coming? When? Tomorrow? Oh, good show. With Johnny and Henrietta? Good for him. I was going to get a man to ride down for our mail tomorrow. Will you bring it in, and take ours out? Good show. The river's low at your place too, then? Sister Hendrie thought we'd never have visitors dropping in. What *are* you trying to do, Juliana?'

'Trying to get the phone off you so I can disabuse this Rebecca's mind of what you've been implying.'

To her surprise he let it go. She said, her tone as crisp as she could manage, 'I think you must be Rebecca Fordyce. Mr Ramsay told me about you and your husband, Darroch, isn't it? I must tell you not to take any notice of what Mr MacNair says. Till now we've not even been on Christian name terms. He was dead against me coming up here, didn't want his uncle this side of the Rubicon, which I can now understand, but I was more conversant with his uncle's condition than he was and he was fretting for his mountains. Sounds as if you're being flown in—how lovely. I want to get to know as much as possible about the New Zealand high-country, in the short time I'll be here, and I like the women's point of view best.'

Rebecca was still laughing. 'I can see you're putting Thor in his place. Good for you! He was getting above himself. These mountain men are tough cookies ... I know. Well, you'll meet two more of the breed tomorrow. Johnny Carruthers is bringing us across for lunch, in his light plane. He's our lifeline here. Tell Grizel not to fuss, we'll take whatever's going. 'Bye for now.'

Juliana put the phone down and turned to look at Tulloch, back in the chair, with it tilted back. She'd never seen him like this, nonchalant, daring, unrepentant. 'Take that outraged look off your face, Juliana. It doesn't become you. Adds years to you, and could lead to premature wrinkles.'

'None of which worries me one jot. You must be mad! Neighbours are the same the world over, even if these are miles away. You——'

'We've been on metric measures for years in New Zealand,' he reproved her. 'It sounds even further in kilometres. They're twenty miles by road. That's thirty-two kilometres, but only seven if a crow was flying it ... through the riverbed and up the Pass. I mean Thunderclap Pass and Calamity Valley. I'll take you through riding some day; you did say you could ride.'

Juliana forebore to tell him that as she was half-Swiss she probably thought in kilometres long before they came to the Southern Hemisphere and said, 'Neighbours relish any item of gossip. I can imagine Rebecca getting on to Dragonshill and Heronscrag and Pukewhetu ... they'll have me married to you, by conjecture, in a brace of shakes. For someone who was so putting-off when it was first mooted that I should look after Mr Ramsay up here, you're the giddy limit!'

'I should think the word would spread even further. You've left out Rütli Meadow. Henrietta and Johnny would enjoy a spot of gossip like that.'

She seized on the name. 'Rütli Meadow? You mean named after the Field of Rütli? The Runnymede of Switzerland? The Cradle of the Swiss Confederation? How does it happen that a homestead as remote as this ... in the Antipodes ... has a Swiss name?'

Perhaps he was glad to stop baiting her and getting hauled over the coals. He said, 'Henrietta and Johnny long ago met up here when they were both lonely kids with parents overseas. Lots of things contrived to keep them apart for years, though they were meant for each other. Then back here, when Johnny Carruthers designed and built the Beaudonais Bridge at Dragonshill, they sorted out the snarl they'd made of their lives. Somehow they discovered they'd each stayed at Brunnen on Lake Lucerne, at separate times, at the

Grand Hotel du Lac. I believe it's right opposite the Field of Rütli. They went off there for their honeymoon and returned to build a Swiss type dwelling, all brown wood and scalloped balconies, on the land he purchased from Charles and Francis Beaudonais-Smith. It's between two shoulders of hill, sloping down to the Lake, and is for all the world like a Swiss meadow. What are you all shining-eyed about?'

'It's just that it's so surprising and wonderful to find something of my other world right here in this pocket of the Southern Alps, my Grossmutter's world,' explained Juliana. 'She lives on the shores of Lucerne, a few miles from Brunnen. I know it so well. As a child on holiday I had my first hotel dinner ever at the Grand Hotel.'

'You grandmother's world? I'd thought the Swiss ancestry far back. You didn't elaborate. Then your mother is Swiss?'

'Yes, Dad met her on a climb.' She amended that to, 'On a climbing holiday.' All of a sudden she wanted to get away from the too-personal. 'But you wanted me to write letters, and if we're getting mail away tomorrow, we'd better get at them. Especially as I must help Grizel prepare.'

'Most of it can come out of the freezer. Casseroles of chicken and venison and veal already cooked are there, and cakes and biscuits galore. You can help re-stock after the visit. I want to get some stuff off to my Timaru accountant for the Inland Revenue. I'll have to let them know you're on the payroll too. I'll want your full name.'

'I'm not on the payroll,' she reminded him. 'This is a holiday.'

'No one who works as hard as you do, even helping Barbie so she can be in the schoolroom, can be regarded as on holiday. I want no arguments. I'd find it tiresome and time-wasting.'

'I'd have thought Mr Ramsay would have had the final say on this.'

'Not any more. He's a wise old bird. His affairs were put in final order, beautiful order, before he went to hospital.'

'You mean he deeded you the full control of the estate?'

'I've owned half of it for years,' said Tulloch. 'Since I was twenty-three. That's eight years ago. My parents had worked here a long time, owning half, or rather paying it off. That holiday where they had the accident was to celebrate finishing the mortgage for the half. The girls, George's daughters, had shares in the other half. That left a third George deeded to me, and I raised a mortgage to buy the girls out. They found it better to have their money out and invest it. They were never likely to live here and work the estate. It was a huge sum, but it won't be mine for another fifteen years, and they'll need to be good years at that. We can incur big losses if we get phenomenal storms. So . . . to return to our muttons, you're pulling your weight and must go on the payroll. Your full name?'

'Juliana Astrid Hendrie.'

'Astrid? Isn't that a Swedish name? Not Swiss?'

'Yes. Mother was called Astrid, named for the young Queen of the Belgians, who was Swedish. The one who was killed in a car accident on the road round the shores of Lake Lucerne in 1935. My grandmother was expecting my mother at that time.'

He smiled. 'Quite fascinating. So you were possibly named for two queens . . . Juliana of the Netherlands.'

She shook her head. 'No, my father's favourite month is July. He said he couldn't name me July, so he did the next best thing.'

Tulloch nodded. 'A pleasant name, especially when associated with the European July. Like little Todd's poem—I mean the one he copied. The summer of vines and sweet briars, glad, golden July.'

Juliana knew a longing to say it wasn't that July she'd been named for, it had been the New Zealand July. The July that had just begun . . . the one with her sunsets aflame on the snows, July with her dawnings of coral and rose, the world that, when Todd Powers had reverted to Fergus Talbot Hendrie, he had turned his back upon.

But she *mustn't* confide in this man. Today was the

first day she'd sensed a softening in him. Because who knew what lay in Todd Powers' eighteen-year-old past? The youth Polly Ramsay had feared might go to the bad.

She said, shaking off the thought, 'I still don't think it's necessary to pay me. It's for so short a time.'

He looked up at her from under those heavy brows, bleached by Alpine summer suns to tussock colour, and said, 'Don't be too sure of that. I heard a long-range forecast today out in the shed, and the next few days are to be fine. Later they urge us to be ahead with preparations for a big snowfall. We could be snowbound.'

Juliana told herself that the odd lift of her spirits was entirely due to the fact that it would give her more time to find out why her father had left the station never to return.

CHAPTER FOUR

LATER Juliana recognised that day as a stepping-stone. She told herself this was because their clash had cleared the air. It was nothing whatever to do with that kiss, with the unexpected turmoil of her own feelings then. Of course not! It was merely because she'd made it plain to Tulloch that she was a career woman. It ought to make for an easier footing.

The stepping-stone idea was her father's. She'd been following him, as a teenager, from rock to rock across a mountain stream in spate. It was a churning mass of white water and the rocks were slippery and far from level. Dad was looking back, ready to act swiftly if she missed her footing. 'Come on, July girl, the next stone will make all the difference. The rest are closer.'

Breaking with Marcus had been a stepping-stone to freedom, deciding to come to New Zealand another. The wish to do so, to find out the reason for Dad's reticence, had been niggling at her more and more. She'd taken the leap and it was paying off. It had been sheer luck that she had landed, after nursing George, right in the sheep station where his boyish attempt at a poem still had an honoured place on the kitchen wall. Perhaps some would call it Providence. Otherwise she could have searched for months, even in this area where every estate owner knew every other one. Finding Tulloch so anti at first had been a very rocky stone, but now perhaps the other steps would be easier.

His antagonism had dimmed the delight she had found in the unexpected chance, but now that she had convinced him she was a career woman, he should look on her as merely on a working holiday.

It was fun preparing for visitors, and Grizel's well-stocked freezers made it easy. There were bread rolls in plenty that would need only heating to crisp them, and lovely mixtures of vegetables, beans, red and green

peppers, carrots, all chopped finely, and with tiny sprigs
of broccoli and cauliflower, that could be taken out
frozen when dinner was nearly ready, and fried in hot
oil; Juliana found they were beautifully crisp that way
and had all the tang of fresh produce. How different
from the old days when, Grizel informed her, with the
kitchen garden ground frozen solid, they had had to
rely on root vegetables, stored in earth pits dug into a
bank, salted-down beans in huge crocks, or dried peas.

As they worked Grizel filled her in with the life of the
first Ramsay wife up here, an epic tale of provisions
coming in just once a year, called back-loading, which
meant the wool-wagons brought them in when they
crossed the river to cart out the bales after shearing. 'It
was more than a minor tragedy to find the sugar
running out before the wagons were due, or the river
rising while they waited on the far side. It was always
sugar. Or treacle and syrup.

'They got in huge stocks of tapioca, rice, sago,
oatmeal, flour, tried to keep their supplies of candles
going, but often having to supplement them with
candles of their own making, always a chancy business
and if made with less than first-grade tallow, giving off
a rancid odour. Then in an area like this, with the
bush—forest if you like—so far from the homestead,
keeping up with the firing took up a terrific amount of
the men's time, hauling the trees incredible distances by
dray and sledge, over rough riverbeds. Harsh, cruel
country, with gallant women longing for the voice and
understanding of another woman. Yet oddly enough all
the marriages here were happy ones. It's legendary by
now. I hope it always will be. I did have fears when I
thought Thor might marry Anthea, but she would have
been so wrong for here. But fortunately it came to
nothing. It was unthinkable to have *her* take Polly's
place!'

Juliana had to subdue the desire to ask more about
Anthea, and said instead, 'You loved your sister-in-
law?'

'I certainly did. So did our mother. She said it was a
dream-come-true to have Polly marry her son. Polly

didn't have an easy life when younger, but she was always the same, seemed to bring sunshine with her as she walked. Or as she danced. She was so full of the joy of life that she had a spring in her step and a lilt in her voice to the last. I can still hear her chuckling over something the morning of the day she died. No wonder George carved what he did on her gravestone.'

'And what was that?' asked Juliana—then a noise in the doorway made her look up. It was Tulloch. He answered for Grizel.

'It's always best to read these words where they're carved. You've been indoors enough, Sister Hendrie, helping Grizel prepare. The sun is dipping, but there's still light enough. I've got the jeep outside. Come on.'

As they left the kitchen, he reached up for a grey duffel coat with a hood lined with scarlet and big wooden toggles, from a hook in the porch. 'It's piercingly cold, button it up to your throat.'

They went out over the cattle-stops and headed towards a foothill that crouched below taller white-shrouded mountains, starkly classical. The headstones weren't visible from the house because the family cemetery turned the corner of the hill, looking towards the northern chain of mountains, so that it lay in sun all day. She guessed that stark necessity lay behind that, something she'd seen in other mountainous regions. When losses occurred in winter, graves were too hard to dig otherwise. Surprisingly there was a lych-gate at the entrance between tall firs, more typical of an English village than a burial-ground on a bleak Antipodean mountainside.

The Little Acre was rimmed with pines and larches but well away from the roughly-hewn track through it, so it lessened the hazard of ice for vehicles. A strange feeling swept over her and she felt comfortingly near her father. She had seen so many solitary graves with him. But these had company. The stones were from the very mountains about them, and the carving, Thor said, had been done by generation after generation of the Ramsay men.

'I'll just show you Polly's for now,' he said. 'I've

already visited my parents' grave today. It's Mother's birthday tomorrow and with the foursome coming, I mightn't make it, with the flowers.'

'With the flowers? At this time of year?'

'Edelweiss. We always keep some at the homestead for that date.'

'How lovely, and how suitable,' commented Juliana.

'Yes, I think so.' He was smiling, not sad, which was lovely.

He took a look at her. 'Didn't you say your birthday was in July, and that's why they called you Juliana? Perhaps we've missed it, though it's early in July. When is it?'

She laughed. 'It's tomorrow, too.'

'Good lord! You should have told us. Never mind, you're having a party as it is. Not often we can arrange visitors so aptly.'

'Oh, don't tell them back at the house,' she begged. 'I'm not a youngster. And at eight-thirty here tomorrow night Mum and Dad will be wafting me birthday wishes from—from Asia.'

They came to a stop at a grave where at one side was a headstone whose deeply incised lettering read, 'Polly, beloved wife of George Ramsay' and underneath it said, 'Her body lies here among the mountains she loved, but her spirit makes laughter in Heaven.'

Perhaps it was only the cold Alpine air that made Juliana's face quiver, but she felt as if it were a revitalising force coming from that other world itself, annulling what men call death. She said slowly, shakenly, 'Seeing that, how could ever anyone have doubts that we're immortal? Thank you, Thor.'

They were in the jeep before he said, 'You called me Thor. Keep it that way. Every time you called me Tulloch MacNair it sounded like a challenge, a battle-cry. We have enough hostility from the elements here without adding to it.'

She wasn't sure how to reply, so she just chuckled. When in doubt, chuckle. A strange man, this. A man who suited his environment. George was delighted at the thought of visitors. 'We'll make the most of it. The

fact that it's the mildest winter on record makes me feel
we'll get it all at once. And these two are favourites of
mine.'

Juliana said, 'You mean Johnny and Darroch? I
suppose you've known them all their lives?'

Thor guffawed. 'You've bowled him out. Look at his
face! I'll lay a monkey he meant the women, Henrietta
and Rebecca. Come on, Uncle George, own up, you old
womaniser!'

George grinned broadly, 'Might as well. Though it's
because of their menfolk I'm fond of 'em. Now stop
guffawing, you'll give Sister Hendrie the wrong idea of
me. I've known Henrietta most of her life. She's lived in
some of the most sophisticated cities of the world, but
never forgot her school holidays up here. She knew
what she wanted. And Rebecca, she's as game as they
come. Haven't known her long in actual time, but that
doesn't mean a thing. Lordy, what a mettlesome piece
she was! Deceived that tough hombre Darroch up to his
neck.'

'Deceived him?'

'Yep, she's got a cousin who's the dead spit of her,
who got herself engaged to his young cousin. Fairly put
the cat among the pigeons, that one—hopeless type.
The cousin cleared off, and Rebecca dashed up here to
try to sort things out. Helluva mess and mix-up.
Darroch mistook her for her cousin and gave her a bad
time. She didn't let on ... too complicated to tell you
why, then to his consternation Darroch found himself
falling in love with a girl who was, he thought, engaged
to his young cousin.'

'But I take it she was found out and all was well?'

'Mm, eventually, but she nearly got drowned in the
Rubicon before that happened, running away. Young
Lennox married the girl he should have married all the
time, and now they run a launch service in a Fijian
holiday resort. Life takes some funny turns. Rebecca's a
joy. I'm glad Polly knew her, even if not for long.'

Juliana said, 'I wish I'd known Polly. The way you all
speak of her makes me feel——' She stopped and felt
the hot blood come to her cheeks. They all looked at

her. George said, 'Go on, Juliana.' Then as she didn't resume he said shrewdly, 'Frightened I might find it too touching? But I wish you would, girl.'

The colour stayed, but she said, 'I feel as if at any time I could come across her, turning the corner of one of the passages.'

George said, 'You couldn't ha' said anything to please me more. Naturally it's the way of it with me, but I like to think that someone who's never known her in the flesh feels that way too. As if the walls here are impregnated with the love she gave this house. Polly was the eldest of a family who were orphaned. She had a struggle rearing them in city flats, to keep the family together. When the last one was launched she married me, and this house, set in the mountain ways, meant everything of security to Polly.'

Juliana smiled at him. 'Not just security, I'm sure, George, but security and love.'

'Aye, true enough. I never doubted that, even though a stupid woman in Fairlie would have had me believe she was marrying me for a home and an income. I made short work of her, believe me!'

At that moment the men arrived for their game of Scrabble. Instantly Juliana's mind switched back to the scene in Thor's office when he'd been scathing about their reasons for coming. She had a feeling he'd sit and watch their reactions and hers like a hawk, and it would be anything but relaxed and natural, but she was mistaken.

He said, 'Well, I've got something to attend to outside. I'll see you later.'

The men were surprised. Young Collard queried, 'Need any help?'

Thor grinned. 'That offer was very belated. You're more heroic than the others, though. I wouldn't dream of spoiling your fun. I don't need any help. There are drinks on that table in the corner . . . and a dictionary. Wish you luck!'

They were amazed to hear the jeep start up and roar off. 'Blimey,' said Jeff. 'How far's he going? I thought he was just off to the harness room.'

Pete Purvis shrugged. 'Perhaps he wants a yarn to Willocks when we're not round. Anybody put a foot wrong about anything? But he said work, didn't he? Oh, attend to something. Well, I guess a boss can please himself. Where are the Scrabble letters?'

George said he'd trot off to bed and have a good read, Grizel went out to the small kitchen. How cosy it was, playing at the living-room end of the big one. The oil-fed stove popped and purred and the big solid logs burned away on the open fire. Amber, a big ginger cat with immaculate white chest front and paws, tried to make herself more immaculate still. 'Beats me where she gets all the spittle from,' said Collard. 'She makes my own tongue feel tired. I keep swallowing.' They all laughed and started the game. Juliana didn't have it all her own way by any manner of means. Time flew. Presently they heard the jeep coming back and Thor's voice speaking to Grizel, then he came in. They had just finished a game.

Jeff said, 'Care to take my place for the next, boss? This'd be a grand opportunity for me to ring my girl-friend. I'll make sure I mark the toll-call on the calendar, boss. May I put it through in your office?'

'Sure, not only will it be quieter and private, but if Gwen heard Juliana's lilting accents, you might have her up here at the double to find out what's going on.' Juliana poked out the tip of her tongue at him.

It was a pleasant evening and it looked like being a happy day tomorrow. Yet before she dropped into slumber, she knew a longing for her own folk and a moment of panic knowing they were among the big fellows of the Himalayas, not one of the safest places on earth.

She was first out next morning. She thought if she was early she could make a batch of fresh scones before the visitors dropped from the skies and that would save robbing the freezer. As she passed her father's poem she stopped, gazed at the lettering, smiled at it and said, 'Good morning, Dad.'

She jumped palpably when a voice behind her said,

'I beg your pardon?' She swung round. Tulloch MacNair!

She played for time, thinking furiously. 'What did you think I said?'

'I thought you said, "Good morning, Dad," but that couldn't have been right, could it?'

She managed a laugh. 'Hardly. I said: "Good morning, Todd," to that bit of framed poetry. I like that poem. It's so unusual to have one on winter in July.'

'Oh, was that it? You said Todd, not Dad. That reminds me, many happy returns of your birthday, July girl.'

'Thank you very much. Are you ready for your breakfast? I peeped in on Grizel, and she's still asleep. I thought I might take her some tea and toast. She works far too hard for a woman her age.'

'She does. I'll help you. She's not one to start without her porridge, though. Say I put that on? It takes only a couple of minutes and you can do the rest.'

It seemed all high-country men could cook. No doubt they often had to when the women of the station were laid low or away. They took George's through as usual; Juliana was still keeping his days up reasonably short. As she sat down to her own bowl of porridge, she saw a neat parcel beside it. Wonderingly, she looked at it.

Thor said, 'The motto of the House of Thor could well be: "We contrive." We so often have to, at the back of beyond.' It had plain brown paper on it. She used her knife to the Sellotape, then stripped off the wrapping. A cardboard box with a transparent lid was revealed, and there, under it, was an exquisite sprig of edelweiss. Her eyes widened in surprise and delight, and she looked across at Thor, a question in her eyes. He answered. 'We can't summon florists to our door with out-of-season violets or orchids, but I thought Mother wouldn't mind sharing her flowers with a girl who has the same birthday and is marooned up here.'

The coral lips parted over the slightly crooked pearly teeth. 'You—you went up to the cemetery last night? On that ghastly track? And no street lights?'

'The jeep has very good lights. There's another box under that. Sorry they aren't in a setting, so you could wear them, but I named them for you, on a strip of cardboard. Do you as a souvenir of the mountains when you're gone from here.'

Juliana opened it. Neatly mounted were beautifully polished stones, rhodonite, jasper, agate, chalcedony, and a piece of greenstone, the New Zealand jade.

'Not all of Thor's Hill,' he said, 'but all of this region.'

'I'll treasure them,' said Juliana. 'The unexpected birthday gift.' She looked across at him and said with an irrepressible chuckle, 'Never in my wildest dreams, at the time of our first meeting, when we were at such loggerheads, could I have imagined you giving me such an imaginative gift, or be wishing me a happy birthday!'

He chuckled back. 'Neither could I have. I realise now though that it wasn't quite like bringing a complete tenderfoot, a city girl, to an area like this, isolated and frightening.'

She looked thoughtful. 'Isolated, yes, one of the solitary places, but never frightening to me.'

He said gravely, 'It *can* be frightening, even to men.'

'You mean when their women or their children are in dire need of medical attention?'

Tulloch's eyes looked reflective as if he looked back on some dark hour. 'That too, but even for ourselves. Like being on one of the top mustering beats. Like being far from the others and in a moment of carelessness, going over a small bluff when a stone rolled under your foot, and lying there with a broken ankle, wondering if they'd find you. Oh, yes, it can be terrifying.'

'How long before you were rescued?' she asked.

'Three hours. The sun was down by then. There was only Wiley Strange and myself up there. We were after stragglers—the others had gone down. He was a little weed of a man, but whipcord-tough, yet certainly not up to my weight. He got me down to the Back o' Beyond Hut by a superhuman effort and got the chill out of my bones. He'd splinted it, of course. He was never the same again—strained his heart, and died a month later. He gave his life for mine, in fact. It was said his name suited him. He was strange *and* wily. But however crooked his life had been, he was a hero. He hadn't a soul in the world, so we buried him next to my parents. Not that they lay there then, but the plot was the MacNair plot. Good grief, let me get off this morbid subject! Good thing Henrietta and Rebecca are dropping in today, they're so lighthearted you'd never know they were mountain wives. Look, we'd better take Grizel's in or she'll be up and she was mighty late last night.'

'Was she? I thought she went off before I did.'

'She sneaked back when you were asleep, for a special job . . . she was icing your birthday cake, took a fruit cake out of the freezer.' The next moment he was adding, 'Hey, that was meant for a happy surprise, not to make you cry!'

Juliana dashed away the tears. 'Over-active tear-ducts, that's all. Grizel is so sweet. I hope she hasn't overtired herself, all for the stranger within your gates.'

Their eyes met, the tawny and the green. Their gazes clung, then disengaged, Juliana picked up the tray, Thor the teapot.

They laughed because Grizel still wasn't quite awake and looked as guilty as an oversleeping housemaid when she realised how late it was. Birthday wishes were the order of the day, from George too, then one by one the Murray children wished her many happies over the phone. Marian said, 'How super, it being your birthday when the Rütli people and the Craigievar ones are coming. Mum's giving us a holiday and we're going to work on Saturday. Bully for you!'

Grizel had determined on a festive meal. Two leaves went in the dining-room table, the cake on a high stand in the centre, iced as if by an expert, which she vowed she wasn't. 'No, I just picked up hints. After all, a minister's wife attends more weddings than most women, and it was useful. Every now and then someone would have a very quiet wedding, and I've always felt everyone should have a wedding-cake to remember, so I used to keep a cake by me and a few decorations.'

Juliana was slightly aghast when she found all the Murrays invited too. Grizel wasn't turning a hair. 'We make the most of every opportunity . . . it leavens the loneliness. I often wish our mother could see how many visitors we get now, especially since Johnny Carruthers settled on the Dragonshill estate. He gets called out so often as a bridge consultant, they decided they must have a light plane of their own and, weather permitting, we see quite a bit of them. So do the other homesteads. We all share some of the running costs. It gives us peace of mind.'

It was perfect flying weather, a clear winter blue sky, with never a cloud. The mountains were sharply etched against it in dazzling silhouette, with the sun striking blue and green lights from the ice-clefts that gashed the glaciers. The ground was so hard they could actually hear Amber landing as she sprang over Joseph, a patchy-looking cat with a coat of many colours as they made their way to the landing strip.

How casual they were, tumbling out of the aircraft as if they had arrived by bus, laden with mailbags and books and crates of milk from Fairlie where they had shopped yesterday, and a few extra perishable stores and a fat package of work from the Correspondence School. Everyone talked at once, as if the day was going to be so short, they must get it all out.

There was coffee ready and hot savouries, then Henrietta, peaty-brown eyes shining, produced a parcel and leaned forward to put it on Juliana's lap. 'Happy birthday . . . it isn't new, but the best we could do in the time. We'd been to Fairlie before we knew.'

Juliana slit the paper and gazed unbelievingly at a view of Lake Lucerne, taken from the far side and looking up towards Mount Pilatus. For a moment the blueness of the lake shimmered before her, then she gained control and said, 'Oh, Henrietta and Johnny, you've given me your own loved picture! I believe you honeymooned there. I can't believe it . . . look, see that sort of notch of brown between those two shoulders of the hills, that's Grössmutter's house, where so many of my holidays were spent. Yes, truly it is. But can you bear to part with this, it must be one of your treasures?'

'It is, but Johnny took it and he has the negative, we'll get another. He frames them himself, from the wood of the Dragonshill trees ... see. Rebecca's got something to match this, only of here.'

Rebecca said, 'I've been writing up these high-country stations for the paper I used to work on in Auckland, so I took several photos in autumn, of Thor's Hill, when the larches were still golden. You'll find it incredibly lovely then, Juliana. But this will give you a preview.'

Juliana said quickly, 'But I won't be here. But how lovely to be able to imagine it like this.' A strange silence fell on them all. Juliana knew as well as if she'd been eavesdropping on Henrietta and Rebecca on the trip over that they had been having a little matchmaking natter. She could tell it even more by the sly grins on Johnny and Darroch's faces. She added, 'I'm here till George no longer needs nursing care, no more. Just a working holiday. My own home is in Scotland.'

Darroch said, 'Do you mean you have a work permit for only that time?'

'No-o, I'm not really restricted.' Then in answer to his querying look, 'My father is a New Zealander, but he left for the Northern Hemisphere when he was just a youth, but that entitles me to stay as long as I want to.'

'That's okay then,' said Rebecca. 'Perhaps the mountains will get you as they got me.'

Darroch put on a mock-offended air. 'And here was I thinking it was for love of me you forsook your city ways! And, my love, if Juliana lives in Scotland and has a Swiss grandmother, she doesn't have to come to the bottom of the world for mountains. She'll have lived among them all her life.'

At that moment the Murray children erupted in, with Barbara following. She was carrying something very carefully. 'I dare not let them carry this.'

It was a jar of pot-pourri Juliana had once admired, one Barbara had made from the clay of the region, and whose contents had filled the winter air with all the perfumes of summer. Barbie said, 'To let you know our gardens are not always bare.'

Juliana's voice wasn't very steady. 'My cup runneth over. Oh, you dear, dear people!'

George said, 'Mine is in a jar too, well stoppered because it "creeps".' She unwrapped the tissue, a tiny phial lay in her palm. 'Gold,' she said, 'raw gold. Is it from Thor's Hill? Your own gold?'

For a moment, quite inexplicably, George looked sad. He said, 'I'm not sure, but it's from this region somewhere. South Island gold, anyway. Now, there's enough of it to make you a tiny pendant. Maybe it'll make you happier than the man who won that gold from the mountains. I'd like to think it was made into something beautiful and lasting. Gold never did any good hidden away.'

Grizel sprang up and said, 'I'm going to bring Juliana's cake in here for her to cut, and Thor will pour us some wine to toast her. There's some fizz in the fridge for the children.'

It was a lovely day, all too short, because the sun would drop so soon, but it was full of laughter and friendship, quip and jest. Henrietta, Johnny and Juliana inevitably talked of Lake Lucerne, of the William Tell country, of the bright blue and red trains that chugged up the steep mountainsides, the lake steamers, the national day of the first of August when there were fireworks on the lake, and hundreds of Chinese lanterns were set adrift on its waters, drifting like fireflies, till dawn. They talked of the sweet sound of the alpenhorn drifting over the surface from the Rütli Field.

Just before they left Thor carried Johnny off to his office to look at some wool samples. Juliana slipped along to get George's pills. The office stuck out at right angles to George's bedroom and the windows there, and in the office, were open a crack.

She paused to take a couple of pills out of the bottle, spilt them on the counterpane and had to pick them up singly. Johnny's voice came to her clearly, 'I wondered if you knew Anthea is at Mount Cook?'

Thor's voice held surprise. 'Anthea? I thought she loathed this area, especially in winter. But perhaps

Cosmo doesn't, and a jolly crowd at the Hermitage isn't like burying oneself at the back of beyond, as she once said. Though I've always felt Fiji or Tahiti would be more in her line.'

Juliana thought Johnny's voice was rueful. 'She's certainly not with Cosmo, that's all washed up, she said. They've been separated for some time, and she's waiting for a divorce.'

Juliana could have told nothing from Thor's voice, 'I'd have thought she'd have clung to him like grim death. After all, *he's* not only got money, he's a city man, I thought tailormade for her.'

Johnny added, 'Thought I'd better tell you. We were dining at the Hermitage and she came across, asked after you and said lightly that she'd like to see you . . . she'd heard I had a plane, how about it? I said no fear, it wasn't a taxi service. It was for work and emergency service. And she shrugged and said then she'd have to face the Rubicon.'

Thor's voice had hardened. 'Thanks, Johnny. She'll find it hard to get here. She'd have to ring us to fetch her over the river, and it's easy to say no. But thanks for the warning. I'll——'

Juliana realised she was eavesdropping, even straining to get every word, and was appalled at herself. She scurried off. But she couldn't quieten her thoughts. Anthea . . . a beautiful name, was she a beautiful woman? Grizel had said it was a blessing Thor hadn't married her. Thor himself had said the woman he'd wanted to marry couldn't take his kind of life. Then, presumably, Anthea had married someone whose lifestyle suited her. Now the marriage had failed. Why? Had she found that money and the kind of life she'd wanted hadn't added up to happiness? Had this Anthea found out she'd made a hideous mistake? That after all, it was the man who mattered? Oh, stop it, Juliana Hendrie, *what can it possibly matter to you*?

When the plane soared up against the westering sun and flew towards it, when it dwindled to a black speck, then vanished, Juliana sighed deeply. They all looked at her, eyebrows raised. She flushed, said, 'Isn't it absurd?

It's been such a happy day I hate to have it end. I feel I've known them for ever.'

Barbara put an arm round her affectionately. 'Of course. Mountain women, especially wives, are like that. Times we meet are so few and far between we leapfrog over the formalities. We get down to basics. They didn't regard you as a stranger. If George and Grizel can spare you tomorrow, Julie, can you come over and help me with this new batch of work? I want to get the older ones busy on their project, and it would help if you take Jemmy through his figures and letters.'

Juliana looked at Barbara with eyes of love—but envied her fiercely. You couldn't see her grizzling about the hardships of life up here. She'd known all the companionship of university life, of teachers' college, of the staff where she had taught later, the stimulation and interest of sizeable classes, theatres, musical circles, debating clubs, the lot. But there was, almost always, an aura of happiness and contentment about her. About Don, her husband, too. How important it was to be the right sort for the solitudes. To even like one's own company. Had Anthea those inner reserves? Had she changed, so that now she could take the life? It could be—she perceived in herself an inner compulsion to wonder about the woman. How stupid! She was here merely on holiday. She belonged to the other side of the world.

That night the man she had at first deemed as hard and tough as his world of tussock, rock and giant winds, put down the paperwork he'd been doing at the kitchen table and said, 'I'm coming out with you, Juliana, for your tryst with your folk. I don't think you should be all alone on your birthday, in these solitudes. Grizel is terrified you're tempted to wander. She feels you're so used to mountains, you're fearless. You might risk what people not used to this sort of terrain would see as too foolhardy by far. A little wholesome fear is good.'

Juliana looked across at Grizel, knitting a complicated top for one of her granddaughters. 'Thank you, Grizel, but you mustn't worry. My father and my Swiss grandfather both taught us to respect the heights, that it's criminal to jeopardise the lives of people who may have to search for you, by your own carelessness. So Thor doesn't have to bother. I go no further than the foot of the terrace. It's still so high above the valley floor there, I feel my thoughts of Mother and Dad go winging in between the river gorges and across the oceans to them.'

Thor said, 'You said to Henrietta there was mail from them, forwarded through your friend Maddie. What part of Asia are they likely to be in right now?'

She was purposely vague. 'Oh, somewhere in India. It's a vast country and they're on the move all the time.'

'Did you have mail ready to give the Carruthers? I suppose you have to mail it well ahead to some place on their itinerary?'

'Yes, our family is used to that. Dad was always in the travel business, and often led parties himself.' (Well, that was fairly true.)

'Did you give them our address and telephone number, because if they're on the move so much, they could always ring you? After all, we're not likely to be off the station just now.'

'Oh, hardly worth while. I'm here for so short a time. Normally we do keep in touch by long-distance calls, but that's when we're all at home. If I stay at the Hermitage when I leave here I'll probably let them know at one of their mailing addresses and they could ring me there.'

Not till she found out why her father had been so cagey about his life here was Juliana going to tell them much about him. People were so curious about anyone as famous as her father, and if there was anything about his early years he didn't want revealed, then she would never confess to him being what he was, or that he had been the little Todd Powers of the poem on the wall.

Thor said, 'It's colder tonight. Put on that track suit you wore the other night, the green one with the elastic at ankles and wrists. Even these penetrating winds can't get up those.'

She came out in it, in stockinged feet, for her sheepskin-lined boots were standing in the hearth. The suit was fir tree green with white fur edgings round ankles and hood and cuffs and it was tied under her chin with scarlet woollen bobbles. Grizel said, 'Dress up in that some morning so I can snap you for my grandchildren—I could have it put on Christmas cards. We had the homestead on them last year. You could do your hair in two plaits and have them over your shoulders.'

Juliana burst out laughing. 'In these colours I'd look like a walking Christmas tree!'

'That's what I want. No one could mistake you for anything but Swiss in that outfit. But you must have plaits.'

Tulloch came across to Juliana purposefully, and she looked up uncertainly. He meant mischief. 'I know what you mean, Grizel. That knot on the back of her head is in plaits today ... one pull and it'll be down.' He tugged the bobble-ties undone and pushed the hood back. His fingers found the tortoise-shell pins she'd used and the plaits tumbled down. The golden hair was parted at one side, but the plaits were even and little tendrils hung each side of her ears. She couldn't help laughing, wrinkling her nose with its line of tiny freckles across it.

Grizel was laughing too. 'Go on out or you'll miss your eight-thirty minute. I wish your parents could see you right now—they'd think they were seeing their little girl of long ago.'

Juliana pulled a face. 'Just as well none of the junior nurses can see Sister Hendrie now! I just don't know what Thor Hill's done to me. It must be you and George ... you treat me like a youngster of the family, and I'm twenty-six today!'

They went out into the starry night and the cold, pale purity of the everlasting mountains ...

CHAPTER FIVE

THEY descended the steps and as Juliana lifted her eyes to those clefts in the mountains beyond which her thoughts and her love went winging, she was glad that this Tulloch MacNair standing beside her knew enough not to speak. There, across leagues of ocean and continent, from some Himalayan camp-site, her parents' thoughts were reaching out to her. The moment ended, she put out a hand to Tulloch.

He turned swiftly, pulled her towards him and against him and she was engulfed in his huge embrace, her face resting against the soft fur of his alpine jacket.

She said instantly, 'Thor, I wasn't looking for this, it wasn't an overture . . . it was just a gesture to thank you for keeping quiet and to let you know it was over.'

She was glad he took her seriously and didn't laugh. 'Juliana, I know that. Devilish, being a woman, isn't it, and afraid of being misunderstood? I recognised that for what it was, but allow me a few natural male impulses. I'm not entirely a man of rock, you know, even if I live among iron-hard mountains! Look up at the sky, girl, and decide if a blaze of stars like that should be wasted! Think of the people in crowded cities who long for a setting like this . . . a world of our own . . . look at the edge of the mountain ridges against that navy-blue sky, and listen to the sound of the river forcing its way through the gorge more than a dozen miles away . . . and realise that in all this emptiness there are just the two of us here. Why waste it, I say!'

Juliana was struck silent out of pure enchantment. This was magic. This was not the dour man she'd first met. He was eloquent. This was a kinship she'd thought she might never meet. Her lips parted as delight flooded her.

The his voice changed and he almost thrust her from him and harshness grated his voice. 'Oh, all right, all

81

right. I'm not the one you want to share this with, am I? Despite the fact you wouldn't follow him into whatever way of life he wanted to take, you're still pining for your ex-fiancé, aren't you? Was it him you were communing with, not your parents? Sorry I thrust my company on you!'

He had actually turned away from her, ready to leap up the steps above him, but she made a wild clutch and restrained him. Then she said calmly, 'Tulloch MacNair! You've got it all wrong. Just because I gasped, you thought I was longing for someone else. Just because I didn't melt into your arms right away, you've taken the huff. It couldn't be further from the truth. It would have been a hideous mistake on my part to marry Marcus.'

'What? Now tell me, what was his way of life that you couldn't take? What *did* he do?'

'What did he do? He was a doctor, but——'

'A *doctor*? Well, wasn't that *your* way of life? Your own profession? It ought to have been ideal. I don't get it.'

She still had hold of his forearm and gave it a shake. 'That wasn't why I gave him up. In fact, his being a doctor almost blinded me to a proper judgment of him. That and his charm.'

Tulloch's face became intent, the lines grooved by wind and weather and experience in his cheeks deepened. 'Blinded you to what?'

'To the fact that he'd make an unfaithful husband. So I turned him down.'

'What made you realise that?'

'Because he was an unfaithful near-fiancé. And his life out of professional hours consisted of parties where there was too much drink—and cheap talk—and social snobbery. I guess if I gasped, Thor, it was because what you said was the opposite of cheap. It was sheer poetry, the sort of talk I was used to in our own family circle.'

This time the lines deepened with smiling. He said softly, 'You aren't averse then to a little poetry? . . . and perhaps a little romance . . . like this? . . .' she was brought close again and he bent his head. Again she

was aware of the leaping pulses she had known
yesterday afternoon, a heart that seemed to thud
against her ribs, a sweet possession taking her over.

She opened her eyes a little, saw the Milky Way in all
its splendour above their heads, and thought dazedly:
'This is Tulloch MacNair kissing me ... and I'm
finding in his kisses what I never found in Marcus's.
And the world I've known and loved best, the world of
mountain and river, snow and valley and the lonely
places of earth, is all about me' ... then she closed her
eyes again under the rapture of it.

He released his pressure on her mouth, trailed his lips
across her cheek in a fleeting caress, then opened his
own eyes and looked down on her, laughingly. 'Those
absurd plaits, Rapunzel! They make you look sixteen
and, as I said yesterday, I don't want you to look so
young. I like a woman to be more mature than that.'

Juliana released herself, brought up a hand to each
plait, twitched them scornfully over each shoulder and
said, 'I've been thinking for days I'd like my hair short
again. Since I've been riding up here I'd love a good
gallop with the wind streaming through my hair.
There's nothing to compare with it.'

To her amazement Tulloch was horrified. 'It would
be a crime to cut it. Thank heaven there's not a
hairdresser within reach!'

She giggled, glad to lessen the intensity of feelings
that had shaken her so, flaring up between them like
that. 'It wouldn't be a crime. It would be very sensible.
After all, Rapunzel is a back number. Women don't
need to let their hair down for a rope so that princes
can rescue them, any more. Wasn't that the maddest
fairy-tale of them all? I can almost feel the hair being
pulled out by the roots. I wonder what weight that
prince was!'

Thor took her hand. 'Come on, that's a very
unworthy thought for a girl who was appreciating
poetry just a short time ago. Most prosaic! Besides, it's
time you were in bed. It's been a big day.' The craggy
face looked suddenly whimsical. 'Or do you think me
mad saying that? Four people drop in out of the skies

and I call it a big day—made it sound as if we shouldn'
sleep tonight for sheer excitement.'

They were climbing the stone steps towards th
lighted house. Juliana laughed like a child. 'I did find i
exciting. I can't imagine a lovelier birthday. From star
to——' she stopped.

He looked down on her. 'Don't be so begrudging
Why didn't you say "from start to finish"? I'd like t
think you enjoyed that short dalliance under the stars a
much as I did.'

She knew she had, but when she finally climbed int
bed she wondered a little ruefully if he wanted her t
understand it was just that and nothing more ..
dalliance? A little lighthearted lovemaking with the onl
unattached woman on the station!

Three nights later George had his nightmare. Whei
Juliana heard the muffled gasps and calls she was deep
in sleep herself, but came instantly awake in the way
familiar to nurses and mothers.

She leapt out of bed and rushed in, switching on hi
bedside light, fearful he was having a heart attack. Ther
she realised what it was. He was muttering: 'Polly ..
Polly, strike out, strike out, I'll get you. I'll get you!'

Juliana bent over him, grasped his flailing hand
firmly, and spoke to him gently. 'Come on, George ..
it's just a nightmare. Wake up, everything's all right
George ... wake up!'

Suddenly he came up out of it. Perspiration was o
his brow, sheer terror in his eyes. Then his eyes focuse
and he recognised Juliana. 'Oh, Nurse, thank heaven! I
was the old, old nightmare. Soon as you got hold of my
hand it was all right. Oh, the weight of that thing on my
arm! And all the time Polly getting swept away by the
current! It's always the same dream.'

'It's a recurrent nightmare. Do you want to tell me
about it?' She knew he mustn't sink back into sleep too
soon or he'd re-dream it. She said gently, 'It's quite
common, you know, after losing someone so near, so
dear. You dream they are out of reach. I'll sit beside
you till you're quite wide awake and till you drop off

again. I snatched up my wrap but didn't stop to put it on. I'll put it on now.' She shrugged on a soft rose-coloured velvet dressing-gown.

George's beautiful blue eyes were clear now. He said, 'It's certainly a nightmare, but not being able to reach her was real, long ago. It was way back before we had four-wheel-drive trucks to ford the Rubicon. Horseback or dray was the most common method, or by gig if it was a social affair and we were dressed up. I remember Polly had a new blue dress and a hat all little flowers, perched over one eye. We were going to a wedding, but halfway across one wheel of the gig collapsed and we were thrown into the water. Unfortunately my side of the gig pinned my arm down. I was against a shingle bank in the middle, quite shallow, otherwise I'd not be telling you this now. But I saw Polly being bowled over and over in the fastest current. I knew she was a good swimmer, and thought she must have hit her head, so I was struggling and shouting and when I thought it was all up with her, the maddened horse dragged the gig off my arm and Polly did strike out for the shingle bank. I reached her, we sat there with the river washing over our legs, then we managed to ford it on foot, back on this side. We reached the house, the men came to the ford on horses, went through and managed to cut the gig horse free—he'd stopped on the other bank—and led him back.'

Juliana shivered. 'No wonder you still have night-mares about it! And poor Polly had to forgo the wedding.'

George began to laugh. 'Not Polly! She'd looked forward to it for months. She changed into her second-best frock, and we rode over the damned river. We had an old flivver in the garage at the other side, and we got to Fairlie as the bride arrived. Polly wouldn't let me tell anyone in case the bride got the shivers thinking of what might have happened.'

'Dear Polly,' said Juliana affectionately. 'Now, George, settle down. There's enough glow yet from the fire to keep you company. I'll put this light out, and sit with you awhile.'

He dropped into a relaxed sleep. A quarter of an hour later George put out a hand gropingly and said 'Polly . . . Polly, are you there?'

Juliana didn't hesitate. She put her hand out, took it in his, carried it to her cheek, rubbed it against hers and said on a thread of sound, 'I'm here . . . goodnight George,' kissed his hand and laid it back on the turned over sheet. George turned his head to one side and slipped into dreamless slumber, happy and comforted like a child.

Juliana rose, moved silently towards her door, the communicating one, and came to a stop as she saw Thor standing in the one that led into the hall. He put a finger to his lips, then beckoned.

Juliana knew alarm. What if he misunderstood, what if her caress had revived in him the suspicions he'd had of her when he first knew she was accompanying her patient to the back of beyond?

She slipped into the hall, dimly lit by one wall-bracket, and said defensively, 'He thought I was Polly, so I pretended I was. And I don't care what you think, so there!'

'Oh, you chucklehead!' he said, and gripped her elbows to shake her. 'I know I thought all sorts of things about you in Timaru, but I know you by now. Besides, I was there from the start—I reached the hall door as you got to George. I admired your technique. It was bang-on. I didn't make my presence known because you were handling it so well I didn't want to startle my cousin. You know, it was rather . . . idyllic . . . to watch. I don't think George will know in the morning if he dreamed that comforting gesture or not.'

The relief at not being misunderstood shook her. Tulloch said in a whisper, 'I hope your dreams are as sweet as George's. You deserve that they should be. Now, off to bed . . . if Grizel investigates and finds you in those delectable garments and me in my pyjamas goodness knows what she'd think!'

Juliana lifted her chin a little to look straight at him, said, 'Not Grizel. She'd ask what had happened and we'd tell her and she'd believe us.'

He nodded. 'And you'd be right, she would. Goodnight, Juliana Astrid Hendrie.'

Their phone rang before breakfast. Thor answered. 'Oh, we'd be very glad to see you, of course,' was his answer to the voice that crackled a bit as their phone often did. Though you'd be wise not to stay too long. The weather's supposed to deteriorate by the longer term forecast—but anything that brings television nearer is welcome. You know the airstrips, of course. What time are you setting off? Good. Look forward to seeing you.'

He sat down and attacked his bacon. 'The TV fellows. They've been up at the Hermitage, tracing a fault there, and though they can't do much here at this time of year, they thought a check of certain things, in addition to what they've done already, would speed things up come spring. They'll be here soon, will be staying the night, unless I can get them up to Beacon Point and back in very good time. Any chance of some mutton sandwiches and a couple of flasks? I'll take them up the dry river-course in the jeep. If they make good time they'll take off again late afternoon, but I doubt that.'

Grizel and Juliana set to work, put in some slabs of cold pie, made of venison mince, and some hardboiled eggs over from yesterday, as well as the sandwiches. Thor said, 'How about coming, Juliana? You've not been as far as Beacon Point? You won't take up much room even if they've got a fair bit of gear with them.'

Grizel cut across her objections. 'Time you had a day off. Get into that track suit—it's even colder at the Point than here, it's so much higher. And though you'll have to do some climbing if you go right up, you'll need warm clothing.'

Thor said, 'I won't bring them up for morning tea, the airstrip's well on the way. We'll have some halfway up. Chuck in another flask, Grizel. We can't waste time these short days.'

Juliana was surprised at the delight, the elation that was taking possession of her. Last night's incident had

made her happily confident that barriers were being
swept away.

She appeared in her green and white and red, cheeks
glowing, warm gloves on, climbing boots in her hand.
They went down to the airstrip, saw the small plane
turn into the wind and make a perfect landing. Out
stepped not just the two male figures expected but a
third, a very feminine one despite the trousered legs.
They were such elegant trousers, black, steel-buckled
about the waist over the bloused jacket, and with an
emerald-green scarf tucked in and gloves to match. The
ski-cap was white against the smooth black hair parted
in the middle and drawn severely back. Long golden
earrings swung from her ears and ought to have looked
ridiculous in this setting but didn't. Her skin was pale,
flawlessly matt, and her eyes were almost black. Every
feature was exquisite and when she spoke her voice was
husky, provocative, seductive. Any woman would envy
her that voice; how anyone could get such a caress in it
Juliana couldn't imagine.

What on earth were those technicians thinking of to
bring a creature like that here? Was she a wife of one of
them, a girl-friend? Her first words dispelled that. She
moved towards Thor, held out her hands and said,
'Tulloch ... how wonderful to see you after all this
time!'

Juliana didn't need to be told this was Anthea. Her
heart plummeted. She'd never heard Thor's voice like
this, controlled, expressionless. He didn't even say her
name, just, 'Look what the wind's blown in! I did hear
you were at the Hermitage. Persuaded the lads to bring
you, did you?'

'Too good an opportunity to miss, darling. I overheard
them on the phone and thought it providential—saved me
all that bumping over that ghastly road to the other side
of the river, and the hire car firm wasn't really keen on
having their vehicle left out in an unlocked garage in the
wop-wops. What a glorious morning, if cold. I hope
Grizel has the kettle on.'

Tulloch said, 'Better go up and see. Our morning
tea's packed in the jeep. We're having it en route, can't

afford to waste any time today. This is Juliana Hendrie. She's going with us.'

Anthea swung a sizeable weekend bag at one of the men and said, 'Just pop my bag back in the plane, will you? I'll come up too.'

Thor's lips set in a straight line. 'Sorry, can't be done—no room. The chaps have their gear, of course, but apart from that, I want to bring some stuff down from Hurricane Hut on our way back. No chance at all.'

Anthea made a last bid. She smiled sweetly at Juliana. 'Perhaps you're staying here and will have the chance to go again. Would you mind if I——'

Thor cut in. 'Juliana's coming. She's very interested in this television project. It concerns her very closely, of course, seeing she'll be here when it first operates. Go on up to the house, Anthea. I'm sure you'll get the warmest of welcomes from George and Grizel!'

Phew! No one could have missed the sarcastic inflection. The technicians looked a little uncomfortable. Juliana couldn't help but admire Anthea's sangfroid as she laughed and said, 'Springing a surprise doesn't always pay off, does it, but I'm sure I can break the monotony for George, at least. I'll look forward to seeing you tonight, Tulloch.'

He said, 'Be sure to be ready to take off as soon as we return.' Anthea swung her bag carelessly and began walking towards the house some distance away.

'Right,' said Thor, the tussocky eyebrows down, 'let's pile in. This is great, chaps. I feel it brings the venture nearer for us. It will bring the world to our vision as well as our hearing. Just as well it's been a freak season—normally a trip like this wouldn't be possible. We had that very early snow, then this long, dry sunny spell. But we've not had it all yet, I'm sure.'

Juliana's spirits rose. Thor had said she'd be here when the television transmitter was established. Was that just a deliberate pretence to foil Anthea's attempt to take her place on this trip, or wishful thinking? She didn't know. Meanwhile she was here, with Thor, and Anthea was with George and Grizel. The poor darlings!

The air was like wine, the outlines dazzlingly clear as if etched with a crystal pen. Across the floor of the valley they sped on their lurching, rattling way, grinding over the flattened boulders of stream-beds, dry now till those snows, locked up in the matrices of the mountains, should yield to the suns and rains of the alpine spring and send snow-melt waters along these scoured-out formations to join the Rubicon and swell its braided channels to a turbulent river, bank to bank.

They rounded a bluff that formed a shelter from the piercing wind from the sou'west and enclosed a curve that faced the sunny north. 'We'll have our coffee here,' said Thor. They drew to a shuddering halt.

They piled out, surrounded a huge stranded rock that had a table top to it, set out the mugs and buttered scones and some ginger gems Grizel had packed. What an appetite this air gave you ... Thor took the empty flask and strode off to the stream, saying over his shoulder, 'This is the best water in the world, we might make ourselves a fresh brew up at the Hut.'

One of the men said in a quick low voice to Juliana, 'Say, did we make a bluey bringing that Mrs Rosenby with us? She made it damned hard to say no to her—said she was due here for a visit and how much more convenient for everyone it'd be if we could take her in. But MacNair certainly didn't put the welcome mat out!'

Juliana felt embarrassed, but had to answer. 'Oh, I gather she used to come up here but wasn't the most popular—she thought the life a bit crude. But it'll be okay, not to worry. Don't say anything to Tulloch.' They seemed grateful for her frankness.

When they reached the part where the hills began to rise they ground up quite a steep grade till they reached a small hut, nowhere near as big as some of the shepherds' huts built in strategic places on the station. This looked brand new.

'It is,' Thor answered Juliana. 'If technicians are good enough to spend time up here fixing this for us, I wanted to make sure they never got caught out without shelter either in installing it or repairing it in time to come. Another hut's always handy anyway, in terrain like ours.' It had just two bunks, a tin-lined chest with dark blankets stored in it, to keep them from the unwelcome attentions of the blowflies in summer, a cupboard with a few cooking utensils, tinned food and dried milk, tea and coffee, and a rough fireplace with bars across to stand pans on. Just a survival hut, but Juliana was suddenly swept by a longing—to spend a night up here, with Thor as her husband. She almost felt as if the desire was mirrored on her face and turned away from the men. Brushwood, tinder-dry, and knouty logs were piled up in one corner, and her vision was of that fire with leaping flames, the cold night outside, and inside, the two of them close to the hearh in those rough-looking chairs made out of *manuka* logs and covered with deerskins.

Tulloch said to the technicians, 'I've got some stuff to stow away here, you go on up. Juliana and I will catch you up.'

As soon as they were alone he said, 'I hadn't banked on this, Anthea turning up. I suppose you've realised she was the one who couldn't take the life?'

'Yes, I did. You'll not want to know how I knew. Grizel said once thank goodness you didn't marry Anthea—that there'd always been a tradition of happy marriages up here and Anthea wasn't the woman for the mountains. You didn't misunderstand my actions last night, so I wanted you to know that was all that was said. I wasn't gossiping or being curious.'

The granity look softened. 'Thanks, I appreciate straight-from-the-shoulder talking. That's a thing Anthea isn't capable of. I was a fool to fall for her all those years ago. She has the nerve of the devil himself! I was terrified you were going to be noble and let her take your place today—though I'd have botched that somehow. That's why I trotted out the piece about you having a personal stake in getting TV up here.'

Juliana's spirits fell with a thud. Not wishful thinking on his part, Juliana, you idiot, not wanting you to stay on when your nursing job is over, just wanting to score off the woman who had spurned his sort of life. Don't delude yourself.

'Right, let's go,' he said. 'I knew I could rely on you. Keep it up, won't you? Even a tough high-country man needs protection when it comes to the deadlier type of the female of the species.'

She didn't bother to answer, just pulled on her gloves again. She was surprised at how much preliminary work had been done and guessed it had been some job hauling these materials up to the site. They were there an hour and a half, then clambered down to have their lunch, standing outside the hut for it with their picnic set out on the bench outside, entranced by the view.

This gave almost the full range of the estate, a sweep of vast valley floor gouged out by glaciers in the Ice Age, incredibly old, and in two sides of a triangle surrounded and guarded by glittering peaks of unsurpassed beauty. The third side of the triangle was gashed by the riverbed of the Rubicon as it cut round miles behind the homestead, to sweep close at the crossing.

She had the strangest feeling she had seen it before, that it had lain here all those ages, waiting her coming. Oh, how absurd! But you've never had that feeling about any of the mighty ranges and valleys your father has taken you to, she told herself. They were just heights to be climbed, areas to be explored. This was different.

They packed up and descended to the lower ground. 'Have you got much stuff to get from Hurricane Hut?' asked one of the men. That hut was lower, but caught the full force of the nor'westers.

Thor grinned unrepentantly. 'I've none—that was an excuse; didn't want to bring the lady. Most ungallant, but that's the way it is. Don't feel bad about it—you weren't to know, and she's hard to resist when she sets her mind on something. Besides, it's the done thing up here to offer hitch-hikes by air. We're making good time, and I know you'd like to get back today, so we aren't stuck with her.'

They laughed, relieved. 'Thought we'd made a real bluey, but if you can take it like that, mate, we needn't feel bad.'

Juliana's spirits rose again. She wasn't usually so
mercurial. What was the matter with her? Oh, she
knew, that moment of revelation in the hut when she
had pictured the two of them there, had been
inescapable. She mustn't . . . she mustn't. She was here
to find out why her father had never talked about his
life here, then to pack her bags and go. If only there
was some old character in the district who had been
here when Todd Powers had left when he was eighteen
. . . and changed his name back . . . and had cut off all
contact with the place. Yet he must have loved it.

They came back to the airstrip area, stowed the men's
gear back in, drove off to the homestead for Anthea.
George and Grizel appeared on the terrace as if they'd
been waiting and came quickly down to save them
driving right up. George said, 'You're wanted back at
the Hermitage tonight if you can possibly make it.
Some more faults have developed. Can you do it?'

'Can do. I'd decided to anyway; we got through very
quickly up there. Where's Mrs Rosenby? We must get
cracking right away.'

George and Grizel looked guilty. 'She's gone off for a
walk.'

Tulloch MacNair stared. 'Anthea? By herself? What
the devil for?' He added, 'And how far?'

'Too far to be back quickly. Said she wanted to walk
to the Lookout by the Old Ford—she said it was her
favourite view when here. Beats me, I didn't think she
had a favourite anything then. She took it into her head
while I was on the phone, and by the time I'd finished,
she'd told Grizel and was gone. I took off after her in
the truck, when I knew you'd have to go back tonight,
but she must have taken that short cut through the
Douglas firs. Couldn't find her at all.'

Tulloch swore, then shrugged. 'Well, can't hold you
chaps up. If she was delayed, it could be a less than safe
flight. It would be just like her to have sprained her
ankle. I'll take her across the Rubicon tomorrow and
down to Tekapo and she can damned well get the bus
back to the Hermitage from there. If we miss it she can
stay the night down there.'

While he was running the men to the plane, Grizel let go. She was furious. Juliana boggled; she'd never seen Grizel like this. George sat at the kitchen table, eyes a-twinkle, while Grizel raved and Juliana continued staring. Grizel finished, 'There . . . I've got it out of my system!'

Juliana couldn't help it, she leaned back and laughed helplessly. 'Grizel, I *do* love you! You're so unexpected. My idea of a minister's wife is one who'd find an excuse for the very devil himself . . . like ours back home. But this is so satisfying. It makes you human. I could imagine you feeling you must show the usual high-country hospitality and being unnaturally polite and not letting her get under your skin one bit. No wonder Anthea took herself off for a walk!'

Grizel thumped her fist on the table. 'It was nothing of the kind. My hearing's not so good now, but believe me hers is as sharp as a cat's. When George told me that the men were to go back tonight, and I realised how his answers would have given it away I knew full well that that . . . that that——' George cut in irrepressibly, 'Watch it, sister dear! There are *some* words that are taboo to even such a minister's wife as you. Just say that Jezebel of a woman.'

His sister swept him a scornful glance and rushed on, 'That that woman was bent on putting as much distance between herself and the homestead as was possible so she'd *have* to stay the night.' She added, 'But at least it seems as if Thor's not minded to make a damned fool of himself twice.' She paused, then said, with a direct look at her brother, 'George and I were so thankful you were here. She's already very uneasy about you—we saw to that.'

Juliana's eyes widened apprehensively. 'Grizel, what have you been up to? Tell me! George, if she won't, you must.'

Grizel said like a naughty child. 'It wasn't me. It was him.'

Juliana said sternly, 'Now come on. It wouldn't be George.'

George remarked drily, 'What makes you think I'm

not capable of throwing my own spanners into the works? I just sang your praises, forbore to mention that you came up here nursing me, though I did say you were a fully trained Sister, that it was a great comfort to me and Grizel at our age to have someone with your experience at hand in case of illness. That we'd postponed our retirement in Fairlie indefinitely.'

Juliana looked at them accusingly, then crumpled into laughter. They were all three still laughing when Thor came back. 'I didn't expect you to be so merry. I thought by now you'd be able to cut the atmosphere with a knife. I don't find it at all funny.'

They sobered up immediately. George, seeing the two women couldn't seem to think of any excuse, said, 'It's my wicked sense of humour, Thor. It tickles me to have Anthea turn up and find anyone as lovely as Juliana here. I purposely didn't say she came up here as my nurse. She thinks we've known her some time and I was lucky to have a friend nursing me in Timaru. The women found it funny. Now where do you think Anthea's got to? It's not the sort of country to be wandering over alone.'

Tulloch's voice was drily amused. 'She'll turn up as soon as she's sure the plane's gone. Much good it'll do her. It's over the river with her in the morning.'

Juliana knew great relief. Only dinner and breakfast to get through. 'What room will she sleep in, Tulloch? I'd better go and make up the bed.'

Tulloch's profile was as craggy as one of the forbidding cliffs they'd passed on the way to Beacon Point. 'She can have the little one the other side of the work-kitchen. But *you* aren't making the bed up. You can switch the blanket on to air it, but just put the sheets and pillowcases on top of the bed and a couple of towels and she can make it up herself.' He stalked out.

They were left gazing at each other. Grizel said, 'Help me with the vegetables. There's a venison casserole in the oven. I'll pretty it up when I go to serve it, with crystallised cherries and blanched almonds, to show her we can put on a meal not far off the Hermitage standards. We had those crumbed sweetbreads over, didn't we? I'll make a sauce and put them on our scallop shells in the oven for an entrée. What about pumpkin soup with a swirl of tinned cream in it, to start with, and as we've a few lemons left, any chance of you making that lemon sponge soufflé dessert you produced the other day? Light but elegant.'

Juliana was still inclined to chuckle. 'As long as you can give me a definite time to have it ready by. A soufflé, like omelettes, will not brook delay, it sinks into a soggy mess.'

Thor came back. 'She's coming back now, from the direction of Barbara and Don's. Not from the river—that was a blind. I hope she didn't upset Barbie. Juliana, I want you to wear that bluey-greeny dress you wore the other night. You know, last time the boys came up for a sing-song. I'll go and meet Anthea. Don't want to slap her down in front of you all, but she's going to know I saw through her ruse and that her visit here is going to be of very short duration. Then if she's got anything to tell me, she can get it off her chest.'

Juliana said unhappily, gazing after him, 'I can't help feeling sorry for her. Perhaps she did make a mistake marrying the other one and has been so hideously unhappy she felt impelled to come to see how Thor had made out.'

Grizel looked agitated. 'Don't go all soft on us, for goodness' sake. Compassion in this case will get you nowhere. You're just too nice to be in any way fitted to cope with Anthea's devious ways. Be on your guard, even if it's for so short a time. Run off and change like Thor asked, pop a pinny over it, and you can make the sauce for the entrée and the soufflé then.'

Juliana found herself obeying. Impossible not to wonder what Thor's feelings would be when Anthea had him to herself, which was what she had wanted. If she played for sympathy, would she succeed? What man is proof against a woman he once loved?

She went into the kitchen as Thor and Anthea came in, tall and slim in her bluey-green woollen dress, its cowl-neckline falling softly about her creamy throat, a Swiss leather girdle about her waist that was studded with green, scarlet and white against its black background and fastened in front with swinging golden chains. The smooth golden hair had its tendrils pinned back now with tortoiseshell combs and was swathed up into a knot on top.

Anthea certainly had superb poise, you couldn't help admiring that, because in the mood Thor had been in, he'd certainly have torn a strip off her. She said, as anyone might have, 'I do hope you've not gone to too much trouble. I'll take pot-luck. After two weeks of the Hermitage's magnificent meals I can stand plain food.'

Thor said, 'I hope not too plain, after all *we've* not had that fare. Not that we need it. Juliana's grandmother is Swiss. I'm dying to meet her. She trained Juliana in all her culinary arts. She makes plaited loaves and brioches and croissants for the sheer fun of it. And her apfelstrudel is out of this world.'

Juliana pulled a face at him. 'It's a real Kiwi meal tonight, but Anthea can have croissants on her breakfast tray instead of toast tomorrow morning if she likes.'

'Not a tray,' said Thor ungallantly. 'We'll have to have breakfast on the stroke of seven, out here. We're moving wethers tomorrow, so it'll be a short enough day, Anthea, by the time I get back from taking you to Tekapo. I can't leave it all to the men. Juliana, I believe you wanted to be with us when we move them. It'll be fun for you. But you're coming to Tekapo with us first. So seven sharp, Anthea, and your bag packed tonight. I want you over the river by shortly after eight.'

'If that river doesn't rise,' said Anthea mockingly but lightly.

Juliana looked down on the eggs she was beating, to hide her dismay. How foolish to think it might happen. The sky was as clear as ever, the forecast good. By tomorrow Anthea would be gone.

CHAPTER SIX

JULIANA decided it was up to her, the one person in the house who hadn't known Anthea earlier, to lighten the atmosphere. The others had a shared experience of the trouble and heartbreak this woman had caused, and it was evident they couldn't forget it.

Tulloch had been their young kinsman, just recovering from the loss of his parents, so he would have been vulnerable, in love, finally disillusioned and bitter. So George and Grizel were on the defensive, antagonistic. A wave of sympathy for the young Tulloch swept over Juliana. He then wouldn't have had those rather grim lines carved down his cheeks. He would have been eager, boyish, full of faith.

But now Anthea might have changed. She might have come back hoping to find someone who still cared. Tulloch was making it brutally plain that it was all finished. In some ways she admired that. A lesser man might have been moved at the sight of his former love, but to Thor, she was another man's wife still. Nevertheless, it must have taken a certain kind of courage for Anthea to come up here to investigate. It wasn't as if it were a populated area where a woman in that situation could call, casually, assess the situation without losing face.

Juliana showed her the little room Thor had said was to be Anthea's, saying lightly, 'I've switched the radiator on and the electric blanket. If you want to freshen up and change, you could just make your bed up after the meal. The bathroom is just along——'

She was interrupted. 'Of course. I know every inch of this place—I'm not a stranger. I always had the Tekapo room when I was here before. Much more convenient. It has its own bathroom.'

Juliana kept the light tone, 'Yes, it's a beautiful room, isn't it? And the hangings are exactly the colour

of the lake waters, that sort of milky turquoise. But it's
being done up, the curtains are down, and whenever the
men can spare the time, they're stripping the wallpaper.
You know how it is on a farm ... the men start doing
inside jobs in winter, but urgent chores always come
along, and the papering stops halfway through. This
was fated from the start with George taking ill, Grizel
having to stay down in Timaru so long, and so on. It
needs a woman to egg the men on.'

(Thank heaven that room *was* being done up, because
she'd an idea Thor wouldn't have put Anthea there,
anyway. He'd no intention of having her find life up
here at all comfortable.)

Anthea had paused in her unpacking. 'How very
awkward that must have been. Did you and Tulloch
stay on up here?'

Juliana didn't allow herself to be ruffled. 'Oh, no, I
was in Timaru too. Thor went to the cookhouse for his
meals. They have a good cook—I don't know if he was
here or not when you were up here. Willocks, a
Tyneside man.'

'Heavens, still here! I remember him. Rather
taciturn.'

'Was he? Perhaps he's mellowed, though the fact that
I did some nursing in the Newcastle Infirmary perhaps
made a difference with me. We talk a lot about
Northumberland.'

'Nursing? Is that what you do? Oh yes, believe
George said so.'

Juliana couldn't help it. 'Well, it's what I've done till
now.'

Oh dear, she was every bit as bad as George, hinting
at a closer connection, one that could put paid to
nursing. She added quickly, 'I did most of my nursing
in London, but I've got itchy feet and nursing is a
profession that can take you round the world. I've
nursed in Switzerland, staying with my grandmother,
and for a short time in India. That was a marvellous
experience.'

Anthea stared. 'And you can take this sort of weather
.. after India?'

'I like variety as well as travel. Though I've got the latter out of my system by now. New Zealand was the ultimate in any case.'

It was amazing how much Anthea had managed to get into that grip that was all the helicopter boys had allowed her to bring. It was evident she'd prepared for more than an overnight stay. But why, when she knew she was being ferried over the Rubicon tomorrow morning, was she unpacking it all?

Anthea said thoughtfully, 'And where did you and Tulloch meet?'

'In Timaru. I'd been there some time before I came up here first. Do you mind if I go now? I'm supposed to be making a soufflé, and I've got the egg-whites to do yet. Grizel will be getting fidgety.'

There, she'd done her best to be cordial . . . but she'd better not trust her luck too far. She might trip herself up. Also, she must warn the others that she'd said they'd met in Timaru, and made it appear she'd been up here before.

Surprisingly, she found Thor chuckling with George. 'Good for you, my crafty old cousin! I think we can reckon you as completely recovered now if you're up to your tricks again.' He swung round and regarded Juliana appraisingly, 'Good girl, you've togged up. How very obedient!'

A flake of colour stained each cheek, 'Well, don't count on my being too docile. I've gone along with this so far, mainly because it's for so short a time, but Anthea is a guest here and I think from this moment on, we should behave normally. I couldn't stand the thought of dinner eaten in an atmosphere of hostility. She may have suffered most traumatically over the break-up of her marriage and be quite different from what she used to be. You've made your position plain, Thor, so let's make it as pleasant as possible for the rest of her stay.'

Thor blinked at her, but before he could speak, George said affectionately, 'I like this little girl, don't you, Thor? She's a lass of spirit, but she's also got a very soft, compassionate heart. All right, girl, we won't upset you.'

Juliana's dimple in her left cheek deepened. 'Oh, George, fancy calling me a little girl! I'm twenty-six and a tall, bossy nursing Sister, as you well ought to know.' So they were all laughing when Anthea came in, clad in a steel-grey skirt, pencil-slim, a sapphire jacket belted loosely over a pale blue blouse, a string of pearls about her throat and pearl bubbles at her ears, accentuating the exquisite pallor of her skin.

Juliana thought: Oh, the poor thing. She might think we were laughing about her. Or that Thor was telling us what he'd said to her, on the track. She said quickly, 'George just called me a little girl, which made me giggle, and I reminded him that I was a tall, starchy Sister who bossed him within an inch of his life in that private hospital in Timaru, and that I can be a holy terror!'

George said, 'It was no use my thinking I could get away with anything just because I knew her so well. All my dreams of having a friend at court faded before her dread authority.'

Juliana finished whisking the egg-whites, folded them in, and slid the dish into the oven. She glanced at the clock and said, 'Now if we serve the soup right away, Grizel, that should be timed to a nicety. There's more to be said, really, for an old-fashioned steamed pudding you can put on two hours before the meal and simmer indefinitely.'

She had to hand it to the others, they managed to keep the conversation going in the most normal way. They asked how busy the Mount Cook Village was, avoided all mention of Auckland, talked of the strange winter it had been, politics, and overseas events.

Not a jarring note was struck till Thor said, 'We had Henrietta and Johnny over here the other day. And Rebecca and Darroch too. You wouldn't have known Rebecca. Juliana got a thrill when she found out that Henrietta and Johnny knew Brunnen on Lake Lucerne. They spent their honeymoon there, you know. It was quite near where Juliana's grandmother lives, and Johnny brought a photo he'd taken, and it actually gave a glimpse of her house. Made your day, didn't it, love?'

Juliana's eyes sparkled at the recollection . . . and the endearment, had he but known.

Thor added, 'Next we'll get Joanna and Matthew over from Moana-Kotuku so you can reminisce about London together.'

Anthea took a spoonful of lemon soufflé, said, 'This is really delicious, Juliana—you must give me the recipe. But let me warn you, they also brought Joanna over to see me. They wanted to impress me with the fact that Joanna, at one time secretary to the glamorous Maria Delahunt of the TV series *and* her adopted daughter, could settle down in another back-of-beyond sheep station and love it. These high-country men are very cunning—to say nothing of deluding themselves into thinking the mountains can cast a *lasting* spell over the women they want.'

Juliana caught her breath in imperceptibly. Of what use had it been to implore these three dear people to behave towards this gate-crasher as if she were a welcome guest, if she was going to throw the gauntlet down like this?

Thor looked bland. Juliana didn't know him in this mood. She knew instant alarm. What did it mean? The tawny eyes danced. 'Oh, Anthea, you're right off beam! Didn't Juliana tell you who she is? Mountains cast their spell over her from her cradle on. In fact, it was probably pre-natal influence. Did your mother accompany your father on any of his expeditions before you were born, Juliana? Anthea, she's Fergus Hendrie's daughter. Fergus and Astrid, her mother, are in Nepal right now, on one of Edmund Hillary's pet schemes for the Nepalese people.'

Funny things were happening to Juliana's knees. To her ears too, for that matter. Her knees were shaking and her ears singing. He knew, he knew! How long had he known? George and Grizel must know too, for not one squeak of surprise had escaped them.

Thor pushed his chair back, went across to the bookcase and picked out a volume Juliana recognised immediately. *The Unconquerable Ridge.* He let the pages spring back under his thumb till he came to some illustrations. He went across to Anthea and said with a note of pride that did him credit for good acting, 'There they are ... Fergus, Astrid, Juliana, outside a rather primitive hospital in Nepal.'

George and Grizel were watching Juliana a little anxiously. She managed to look unperturbed, said lightly, 'That book contains my one and only venture into print. Dad made me write the chapter on that experience, from the nursing point of view. The book was serialised first in a magazine that sponsored an appeal for funds for the hospital. That was just a short experience for me, but my brother Robert finished his medical course last year and will be going out to Nepal soon. Liesel is keeping house for him at the moment in our village back home. He's assisting the local medico. She's marrying a Swiss ski instructor and will be within easy reach of Grössmutter. It's quite ideal.'

She felt she was babbling, but in case the others got tripped up they'd better know about the rest of the family.

'Idyllic, in fact,' said Anthea drily. 'You're to be congratulated, Tulloch. No wonder you fell for her! She's tailored to fit the life up here, isn't she? Not many people are. Did you draw up a blueprint for a high-country wife, then institute a search?'

Thor's chuckle sounded quite genuine and unperturbed. 'Well, it wasn't quite like that, you know. I was head over heels before I even knew she could ski, much less scale mountains or have a famous father. It beats me. If *my* father was Fergus Hendrie the whole world would know. No one in Timaru had the foggiest idea!'

Juliana looked at him quite seriously. 'You *wouldn't* tell everyone, you know. It's all right in circles where you're known, where you grew up, but as you travel about, making your own way, you like to have the people you meet liking you for yourself, not because you have a famous father. Once or twice in London I got asked to dinner parties simply and solely because of my father, not because my hosts had an atom of interest in me. I was even introduced in the main as Fergus

Hendrie's daughter. So I learned to sort people out and kept my own counsel.'

Thor surveyed her as if he were humouring her, indulging her. 'Well, at least you can never accuse me of trying for you because of your mountaineering skills or your relations. I got a real shock when I first called for you to bring you up here and you had skis in your luggage. But it was wonderful finding out!'

Anthea hastily steered the conversation away from Juliana and to other days when she'd visited here. It was meant to exclude Juliana, perhaps to sow a little seed of chagrin, of jealousy. No wonder these dear people had reacted as they did when Anthea dropped out of the skies. She was very feline. Occasionally in nursing quarters you met girls like this ... they spelled trouble from the start, they were made for discord. They thought of little but their own looks, their clothes, wanted the centre of the stage, took other girls' escorts away from them.

Finally Thor said, 'I think we'll have our coffee at the table tonight, not later. Barbara said to come over early, Juliana, because the boys want you to tell them some more stories about tigers and pandas and Abominable Snowmen.'

She only just managed not to show surprise. She felt she hardly knew this Thor at all, the one with the bit between his teeth. Grizel switched the percolator back on and brought out peanut nibbles. 'They go to bed pretty early over there because of Barbie getting them into the schoolroom early. So don't you bother with the dishes, you two. Anthea will help me, then we can settle to the radio, there's an excellent programme tonight.'

Thor said, 'Good show, we'll get cracking. We'll take the jeep because that'll save Juliana changing into trews. If she walked over in that get-up her legs would freeze. This way she can tuck a rug round her. Or I can.'

As soon as they stepped out on to the terrace Juliana began to shake with laughter. Thor looked at her, then joined in. 'Come on, or you'll seize up.' He hustled her down the steps and round to the shed where the jeep was stored.

He took his time tucking that rug round her and under her feet. Finally she protested, 'Thor, it's no distance.'

His breath was warm on her cheek, 'But this is so nice, don't you think? Why shouldn't I take my time? No real hurry, that was just to get away from Anthea.'

She said hurriedly, 'Thor, it's all right playing it up when she's there, but you've made your point, don't keep it up, so there's no need.'

His voice sounded indignant. 'What is there in it for me when I've got an audience? I mean, if I did *this* ...' his lips brushed hers lightly, tantalisingly, 'in front of them all, it doesn't mean a thing. I should get *something* out of it for a terrific piece of acting, shouldn't I?'

She said sternly, 'And you deserve a prize for modesty too! Oh, Thor, stop it. I can't think when you——'

'Who wants to think? It's nicer to just feel. Feel things like this ...' he tipped her chin up, said, 'Sister Hendrie, your chin would be a mite too severe if it didn't have that dent in the middle of it.' His lips touched it.

Juliana put up both hands to push his face away, clasping them about his rough cheeks. He instantly covered her hands with his own, keeping them there. 'That's better—feels nice. You catch on beautifully, Juliana.' She tried to give an exasperated sigh and halfway through it turned into a giggle. 'You're quite, quite mad! When I first met you and you were so against my coming up here I could never have imagined anything like this. You were so dour. You didn't want a woman up here disturbing the men, making mischief! But just because I can't help laughing because it's all so ridiculous, don't think I don't realise you're just using me, and manlike can't resist flirting. Just as well I don't take you seriously. Now, I've got questions to ask, would you sit up and listen?'

'No, I won't sit up. I'll listen like this.'

'You're so stupid, and so maddening!' She withdrew her hands, before he could stop her. 'Now——'

'No, you don't.' He put an arm about her, covered her hands with one of his as she clasped hers in her lap. 'Fire ahead.'

It was no use struggling, though she was dismayed at how little she wanted to free herself. 'Now tell me when you discovered my father was Fergus Hendrie?'

'The night we went across to see Don's slides. You were telling the children their stories while Don was getting them in sequence. He told me to get you or the kids would keep you there all night. You didn't hear me coming and I paused in the doorway because I thought it made quite a picture, the three kids sitting up in bed, eyes like saucers while you told them about finding a mongoose in your camp-bed. Oh, you didn't say whom you were with, but it rang a bell ... I'd read it, in *The Unconquerable Ridge*, I was sure. I tiptoed away, then coughed coming back. You'd finished, shooed Marian off to her own room, and I was dying to get home and look it up to be quite sure I wasn't imagining it. Hendrie isn't an unusual name or we'd have tumbled to it sooner.'

'Why didn't you mention it there and then?'

'Thought you must have some reason for not doing so. I thought I had a fair idea why you hadn't.'

'What was that?' asked Juliana.

He laughed. 'I'm not going to stick my neck out, not yet, anyway. I'll tell you some day.' That had a nice indefinite sound about it, she thought, but accused him: 'That's just being deliberately tantalising! You want me to coax you to tell. Well, I shan't.'

'Suits me. At this delicate stage I don't want things cut and dried.'

'You mean because Anthea is here. Has it disturbed you, Thor?'

He said slowly, 'Would you mind if it had?' When she didn't answer he said, 'Don't get that into your head, Ju. Anything I felt for Anthea died long ago. Apart from that, she's another man's wife, even if she was at some pains to inform me that she's just waiting for her divorce to come through, they must have been separated some time. But I know so well how she can foul things up. It's a kink, an obsession. She just can't bear not to have the full attention of any male within her orbit. I didn't want her upsetting Barbie and Don. She tried to make mischief among them long ago, when they were new up here.'

'Did she? But why? Wasn't that when you and she were . . . um . . .'

'Yes, it was, but then we were at outs over my wanting to stay here. All her life, I believe, Anthea has used those tactics . . . show a man he's not the only pebble on the beach and he'll come to heel! If we only knew, that could be the trouble between her and Cosmo. He's pretty shrewd, the big business type, but a sound fellow. They suit, or would if Anthea had enough gumption to play the role he wants her to play. She's probably botched her marriage by still playing one man against another. I don't know what she's up to, chasing up here, but if it concerns me I'm not playing ball. I've used you shamelessly, I know, but I'm damned grateful. Anyway, we'll be rid of her tomorrow and I thought it wise to keep you out of the line of fire tonight. I'm just not letting her get me, either, into any situation, where you could have doubts of me.'

Strange emotions were taking hold of Juliana, sitting within the warm circle of his arms. She must hold them in check; it was just a game. She said quietly, 'Thanks for explaining it, Thor. You surprise me, you know. When I first met you I'd have thought you'd have been taciturn and reserved about an affair like this— unapproachable even. But this is common sense. I'll go along with it. Now we must get over to Barbie's.'

Barbie and Don were devastatingly candid, horrified that Anthea had had the nerve to project herself into Thor's life again, but relieved to know she'd be on her way the very next day. It was a lovely evening with no jarring notes once they'd talked it out. Thor told them, giving them a thrill, that Juliana was Fergus Hendrie's daughter, teasing her about her secrecy because she wanted to be welcomed for herself, not her father. They thought it endearing that the family had a pact to think of each other at a given time every twenty-four hours.

Barbie said, 'May we come out with you tonight and look towards the gap in the mountains? Later your people may like to know that you had friends about you sharing that moment. You'll be writing to them, of course. Any chance of them coming here? They'd be so at home in this setting.'

Juliana said lightly, 'I'm afraid Dad has all sorts of commitments to honour. I probably won't see them till I'm back home in Scotland.'

She thought Don looked surprised, went to say something, then checked himself. She looked up to see Thor gazing at her intently. She said, to change the subject, 'Was Todd a family name of yours, Barbara? Perhaps a surname you adopted for your son's Christian name?'

Barbara shook her red head. 'No, it was that Polly, hom I loved so much, talked a lot of the little boy Todd wwho wrote the poem on winter in July, that I felt it would give her a thrill to have another Todd here. She fretted after that youngster, felt that the Powers, who'd taken him when his parents died, were kind enough but very unimaginative people to look after a boy of that calibre. He was highly strung, sensitive, artistic. Polly and George would like to have taken him, seeing they had no son of their own. But the Powers were fond of him in an unemotional way, Polly said. It meant a lot to her when he came back as a young shepherd, but he didn't stay long and unfortunately they lost touch. So Polly loved us calling our son Todd.'

'I wish I'd known Polly,' said Juliana. They couldn't know how much she wished it, Polly who'd loved the lonely little boy who had become her father!

Thor and Don began talking of adventures on the station when shearing, mustering, snow-raking. These were true mountain farmers, facing hazards similar to those Juliana's family had known all their lives. Time sped. A magic evening with kindred spirits. Suddenly the last huge log on the fire disintegrated in a fountain of sparks. Thor stood up. 'Time we were going, especially as I'll have to be off early with Anthea. I'm taking Juliana too.'

'For protection,' asked Don, teasingly.

'For company on the return trip,' said Thor. 'You and the men can start moving the wethers. I'll be back to help you before long. I'll dump Anthea at the store. She can fill in the time having coffee till the bus comes.'

The Murrays stepped on to the verandah with them and they all stopped dead. Over the ranges an electrical storm was playing, well back in, but it was an ominous sight to them, versed in the behaviour pattern of mountain storms. Here the air was still and dry, ice-cold, bracing. There, all hell was being let loose in the atmosphere ... sulphur-yellow lights, veridian green, saffron gold, pure fire, and a blinding white that somehow was more evil than all the rest as if the very air was blanched with terror. It was right above the Witches' Cauldron, aptly named, and even as they stared, horrified and fascinated by the lack of sound, the silence was split in malevolence unimagined by people who dwelt on the plains.

'You won't be crossing the Rubicon tomorrow, boss,' said Don. Thor didn't argue. They both knew. They'd been too long in the high country not to be able to predict the rise in the river, as sure as coastal men knew the tides. They were right up against the watersheds. Thor simply said, 'I'll ring the weather office to warn them.' That would give them time to let the farmers know, nearer the coast, to shift stock to higher ground. Here it simply meant their river wouldn't be a silver-threaded network of streams, but would be running bank to bank.

'We're stuck with Anthea,' Tulloch MacNair said. He held out a hand to Juliana. 'We'd best get going before it hits here. So much for the earlier forecast. This is a freak storm.'

By the time they reached the house and garaged the jeep the noise was unbelievable, tossing and echoing from peak to peak, flinging the claps of thunder again and again against gorge and canyon walls. Juliana stopped on the top terrace and turned back for a last look at the spectacular display so many miles away, lifting her chin a little, glorying in the might and fearsomeness.

'Sing glory of winter,' said Thor's voice in her ear, 'Magnificent, isn't it, despite what it entails?' She was glad that in that moment, all unaware, he had linked her with her father, the little boy of long ago. He put an arm about her, said again close to her ear because of the uproar, 'You're a real maid of the mountains, aren't you?'

She nodded, then said, 'And you too, Thor. They nicknamed you well—the man of thunder.' They turned the corner—and stopped dead. The curtains at this window hadn't been drawn. It led into a small cosy sitting-room that when Thor's parents were alive had been part of their domain, something that gave them and George and Polly precious time to themselves. Anthea was sitting in Thor's favourite chair, clad in the most ridiculous garment a woman ever brought to a mountain sheep station in the dead of winter, a turquoise négligé that was diaphanous, frilled, trailing. Even her pose was seductive, leaning back, legs crossed, so that it fell away up to her thighs.

Juliana looked at Thor uncertainly and found his eyes were full of devilment. He bent to her ear, 'She hasn't heard us arrive because of the storm. We'll go back the other way and sneak in by the side door. I'm not minded to play host at this hour, it's too damned silly for words. In our passage I'll say goodnight loudly and we'll both bang our doors. I'll steal out later and ring the weather office from my own office.'

It relegated the whole stupid performance to absurdity. Juliana was a-thrill because it was so obvious Thor hadn't a spark of feeling left for the woman he had once loved. They crept in, performed their goodnight act, and gained the haven of their own rooms.

Thor and Juliana breakfasted together and alone. Thor had been out first and had prepared a tray for Grizel as well as George. He'd taken hers in before Juliana appeared. 'I felt she deserved breakfast in bed for entertaining the cuckoo in the nest last night. It was a shabby trick to play on her, but she was glad to do it for our sakes. I've been up the lookout and the Rubicon is an awesome sight, great trees are being tumbled down so that means it had washed up to the lower bushline on the foothills.'

'How soon before it subsides?' asked Juliana.

'Do you mean before we can ford it? It can't be crossed after a flood like this till the river-grader can make it to here and firm up a new crossing and mark the quicksands.'

She shuddered. 'You won't take any risks, will you, Thor? I mean in your impatience to get Anthea out?'

He smiled, in the way she loved, the strong lines softening the weatherbeaten cheeks. 'I've too wholesome a respect for the Rubicon! I won't risk it even to get Anthea out of our hair. I'll only hope that more weather doesn't come our way to make flying hazardous. If it stays clear I might be able to get a chopper in to take her out, no matter at what cost. But it will only be if the firm can spare the time. Rescue operations come first.'

She enjoyed the breakfast for two. Evidently Anthea had decided the storm had absolved her from that early start and was sleeping in. Thor garbed himself for the weather and prepared to fare forth to see the men. He said, 'No taking breakfast in to Anthea, I'll bang on her door to wake her as I pass and tell her we've had ours. She can make her own. Just leave the bread and those croissants and marmalade out. Well, see you lunchtime. Don't let her get under your skin!'

Anthea didn't get under her skin the way he meant, but all unknowing she delivered a blow under the belt. Anthea showed no resentment at getting her own breakfast, but as she sat having it, said, looking round the room with disparagement, 'Not a thing has changed in seven years! They even still keep that ridiculous poem tacked up there on the wall ... as if there's any glory about winter in these conditions.'

Juliana stiffened. 'They'd *never* want to get rid of

that; not many people are lucky enough to have a poem written specially for their very own homestead.'

'Perhaps not, if you like that sort of thing. Anyway, that kid turned out such a rotter!'

'A rotter? What do you mean? I never heard that.'

'Well, he was. Pinched some raw gold out of George's office when he and Polly weren't here and skipped it—worse than taking money. That gold had taken years to win out of the ground. It had belonged to George's father. There isn't much gold round here.'

Juliana's mouth went dry. She swallowed, said, 'Are you sure?'

'Of course I'm sure. Who'd want to repeat a thing like that if it wasn't true? He'd been away for a holiday and wasn't long back when he asked the head shepherd if he could have a couple of days off—said he wanted to get a tooth looked at in Fairlie. They told him to take one of the horses. It was soon after he left that they missed the gold out of George's office. I think it was when the head shepherd went to pay the men. It could only have been Todd. Oh, don't look so disbelieving, what's it matter to you? Just because you like his verses it doesn't mean he couldn't be a thief!'

'The men set off after him. He had it all right, in his saddlebag. He tried to put up a cock-and-bull story about prospecting for it on his holiday—as if anyone cooped up here ever did anything different from hitting the town and painting it red! Said he'd heard the gold assayer was coming to Fairlie and he wanted it valued, but he wouldn't tell them what area he was supposed to have got it from. They'd liked the kid, so they let him go ... on foot. Served him right. But they said if ever he showed his face again on that station, he would be prosecuted. Wisely he disappeared, and has never been heard of again.'

Juliana said expressionlessly, 'There's such a thing about giving a person the benefit of the doubt. Perhaps he thought things looked so black against him he couldn't risk it. It must be ghastly to be innocent, yet not able to prove it.'

Anthea laughed. 'A born romantic, aren't you? That

happens very rarely in real life. And what could it matter to you? It happened so long ago, and to someone you never knew or are likely to know.'

Those last words burned into Juliana's brain and heart. *Someone you never knew!* Oh, no, it was her *father*, then an orphaned youth, bearing a name not his own, a boy who had had to trudge miles and miles of a road that even now was scarcely worthy to be called a road ... and if he was innocent, sick to his soul. *If*, Juliana felt sick herself. Can one person ever be so sure of another's honesty that they could convince themselves, however wistful, that a certain loved one was incapable of theft or deceit?

The thought haunted her all day, hideously, with nobody within the usually harmonious atmosphere of the homestead of Thor's Hill really at peace. It was going to be an endurance test, having Anthea as a guest, with no way of getting her off the place.

Juliana's mind was a treadmill with questions that couldn't be answered, scurrying round and round in exhausting futility. But one thing she did know. Despite those faint stirrings of hopeful dreams last night, this news had made it impossible for her life and the life of the boss of Thor's Hill ever to be linked together. She couldn't, just couldn't, do that to Fergus Hendrie.

Yet at three in the morning she woke suddenly from a shocking dream where first the waters of the Rubicon engulfed her, then she was marooned on the mountain-side on a shingle fan that was moving, that most dread danger ... it was carrying her remorselessly towards precipices and chasms ... She woke moaning, and suddenly the claustrophobic feel of the nightmares was gone and her mind and heart recognised one thing: *Dad had never been a thief*.

CHAPTER SEVEN

NEXT morning misery rushed over Juliana as soon as she woke. Even though her certainty that her father was innocent was still with her, it didn't alter the situation one iota. If this was the place where her father had suffered the greatest humiliation and injustice of his life, she could never entertain thoughts of linking him up with it again. He must never know she had visited Thor's Hill. She must nip her own feelings in the bud, remorselessly.

The fact that Anthea was here helped rather than made it worse, because despite this howling storm Thor was out of the house most of the time. It was obvious he wanted to be as far from his former love as much as possible, something that should have made Juliana's heart sing, had she not been burdened with the hideous knowledge of why her father had left here. No, not why he had *left* ... why he had been thrown out! Might it have been different had George and Polly been home at the time? Even if they'd believed him guilty, might they have given the youth a second chance? From what she'd heard of Polly she'd have found reasons for such behaviour, a sudden temptation, something resulting from a somewhat deprived childhood. The men just hadn't cared; they'd been too disgusted.

It had been rough justice, taking the gold from the lad, forcing him to walk those ghastly roads to Tekapo where he might have got a lift out. Juliana found herself longing to know where her father had spent that night. Under some tree? Had there been many trees then in that bare region? Perhaps he'd had to sleep in the shelter of some rock, away from the blast of the pitiless winds that either scorched or ravaged with cold the exposed downland?

It wasn't like Scotland where there'd always have been some shelter, a haybarn, an outhouse, a haystack

114

... villages close together. She didn't even know if it had been winter or summer ... would he have been frozen to the bone, perhaps even in danger of dying from exposure, or dripping from every pore with sweat as he trudged across the dry tussocks? How much money would he have had? Would he have been hungry?

Would there have been a daily tourist bus from the Hermitage going through Fairlie, then, and if so, had he the money for the fare? His clothes, other than what he stood up in, would have been left behind. Would he, in that case, as a rouseabout on a remote sheep station, have had a savings-bank account of any kind? Would he have had to go to Fairlie to withdraw it? The thought of that foot-weary distance through Burke's Pass to get there brought her to the verge of tears.

She pulled herself together. Even at eighteen Dad must have been something of a mountaineer. All these men here, who mustered up to five thousand feet on foot, were mountaineers, and were tough and resilient. That wouldn't have dismayed him as much as the knowledge that he'd been judged, condemned, turned off by the men he'd worked with. The men here now were fine types, but judging by some of the tales Thor and Don had been revelling in the other night, many of them of earlier years had been rough hombres, men who turned up for work, volunteered very little information about themselves, lived hard, drank hard, gambled hard and disappeared again when it suited them.

Juliana, desolate at heart, stared out of her window at that cleft in the mountains where at Barbara's home, with affectionate company about her, she had kept a communion of the spirit with her parents, in some Nepalese village in far distant mountains. Round the corner of that terrace, on her birthday, Tulloch MacNair had held her in an embrace that had made her glimpse the world of delight she had always, in her dreams, hoped for. Even the return of Anthea had made no difference to that. This was a fine man, he'd been so splendidly unyielding, quite unmoved by her beauty, her nearness, her obvious desire to enter his life

again. She, Juliana, had been foolish enough to think it
was because of her, the nurse he hadn't wanted up here.

It had its funny side, she thought wryly. Anthea
herself hadn't deliberately sabotaged the attraction
between them, though no doubt she'd have wanted to
do so ... that so fragile-as-yet something that was
stirring between her and Thor. But in one sentence she
had, quite unaware, shattered a dream.

No wonder Dad had never mentioned this place, just
said that after his foster-parents died he'd worked
around on various farms. He wouldn't risk any of his
three children wondering if their father had indeed been
a thief. Suddenly Juliana was sure her mother knew all
about it. She and Dad were so close he wouldn't have
been able to keep it from her. And Astrid's faith in
Fergus would have been unwavering, as constant as the
sun, the moon, the stars, fixed in the heavens.

How glad she was she hadn't sent them this address,
that her mail was still coming through Maddie and that
she was sending her own for Maddie to post. It would
have stabbed Dad with cruel precision to see that
address ... c/o George Ramsay, Thor's Hill, Tekapo,
South Canterbury, on her letter. Thank God she hadn't;
he'd think she was just exploring the tourist area
around Mount Cook like any other New Zealand
visitor.

Well, with Anthea here and the hours Thor and
Juliana could have spent together therefore limited, it
would at least stop what was growing between them
flowering into sudden declaration. Juliane bit her lip as a
longing for just that swept over her. She must clamp
down on even dreaming, it seemed, get on with the
ordinary prosaic tasks.

The storm raged for three days, and George was so
much better and stronger he needed much less
attention. Grizel seemed to want Juliana to spend more
time helping Barbara with the schoolroom work.
Juliana said, when they were on their own, 'Are you
sure, Grizel? I hate leaving you with Anthea, I know it's
a strain.'

Grizel looked as mischievous as a three-year-old. 'I

know, but it'd be far more strain for me to see her with you too much. I can read her like a book and I'm far from sure you can. You haven't had the experience of her I have had. When I think of what she did to Thor once—Oh, I'd better leave that alone. He wouldn't thank me for dragging it up now. Thank heaven he's not minded to play the fool twice. But as far as you're concerned, I'm terrified you'll think her consumed with grief, suffering trauma because of her broken marriage, and you'll let her poison your mind. That sounds like strong words, but they can't be too strong. She was wilful, spoiled, crafty and abominably selfish. I'm not going to risk her spoiling this—this thing—for you——' and Grizel, rarely at a loss for words came to a full stop. Juliana gazed at her. Grizel knew she had to finish that somehow, said lamely, 'I won't have her ruining this time among the mountains for you.'

She knew Juliana knew what she'd meant, but wisely, both of them left it at that. Grizel added, 'But promise me one thing, girl, don't believe anything fully she tries to say, or insinuate.'

Juliana hugged her, said, 'I promise. Well, I will go over to the Murrays. I'm not as experienced as Barbara, but when lessons only need supervision I'm all right, and also, when she's hearing their oral work, I can keep Jemmy occupied. He's an adorable child. He's absorbed a lot already from the older children's lessons. He starts school officially next week when he's five, but he's well ahead. His printing is good already.' She laughed. 'He's also bringing me up in the way I should go! The children were all weighed yesterday and the weights entered in their records. When Barbie called out "fourteen kilos" for Jemmy, I said, "That's a big weight for his age, isn't it?" and added, "What's that in stones?" and he said in the most disapproving tones, "We don't use stones any more, Julie, we even *think* metric these days." Funny how quickly we got into decimal coinage and how slow we seem to assimilate the other.'

Thor's voice from the doorway: 'Well, we use money all the time, the other weights and measures only seldom. Juliana, I've come to take you across to Barbara's in the jeep, the rain's eased a little, but cloud and mist are swirling down from the mountain tops.'

At that moment Anthea appeared. She smiled sweetly, then said, 'If Juliana's going to be across at the Murrays' all day, I don't mind giving you a hand, Grizel—perhaps not with the cooking, most women prefer their kitchen to themselves, but anything else. Unless you'd like me to make those salmon croquettes you were so fond of, Thor, for lunch?'

'No, thanks. I'm having mine with the men. We're having a big day with the chain saws. The wood shelter's full of branches but the blocks are nearly finished and it's a great opportunity when the weather's like this. Pete and Jeff are repairing machinery and giving the big tractor the once-over. It'll save time not to come back. But thanks . . . some other time, if you're here long enough.'

Anthea took it quite graciously, 'In that case Grizel might like me to get on with the dusting?'

Thor said, 'Right, Juliana, let's move. By the way, Anthea, Grizel might appreciate some help with the vacuuming. I usually give a hand with that.' He grinned. 'I'm speaking from a purely selfish motive, of course!'

As they drove off Juliana said, 'Thor, you're a devil! You know perfectly well she'd rather flit round with a feather-duster!'

He chuckled, 'I had another motive. Dusting is silent. I came on her yesterday in my office prying through my papers. I didn't bawl her out—she hadn't seen me. I retreated, then came back more noticeably. She appeared from the doorway saying: "I was going to give your office a quick flick round but thought I'd better not disturb that formidable mound of documents."'

'I locked the office this morning. I don't care what she thinks. It's unusual enough for her to get the idea. I can imagine what she was up to. Having come up here with one thought in mind . . . that of raking over dead ashes . . . she's trying to find out if my financial position has improved. It has. The other night she asked me, rather obliquely, when George and Grizel would be retiring to Fairlie. I said that if George wouldn't even convalesce there it was hardly likely he'd be anticipating retiring soon. That perhaps he'd be like old Madame Beaudonais who opened the bridge at Dragonshill when she was a hundred, and died up here.'

Juliana made no comment, but a pang tore through her. That could have mattered to her once, Thor's inflexible attitude towards Anthea. But not now.

He waited for her to speak, then said sharply, 'No comment?'

He was peering through the curtain of thick mist clouding the windscreen so didn't see her hands tighten in her lap. She said tonelessly, 'I do admire you, Thor, not softening towards her. She can't persist in the face of your unyielding position. She's a strange creature. I suppose she waited till she could wait no longer ... I mean after the break-up of their marriage. Then came down here hoping to find you still unattached and thought you might turn to her again. It hasn't been easy for you.'

He didn't reply at once. They reached the other house and he pulled up. He put out a hand to stop her getting out. His tone was rough. 'Don't sound so detached about it all, so academic. You're too distant by far. I mean, if she came down here hoping to find me unattached, as you put it, then she didn't succeed, did she? Oh, come on, Juliana, you *know* how I feel. I even kidded myself I knew how *you* were beginning to feel. Then Anthea had to happen! And till the rain and fog go I can't get her out by river or by air—it's damnable! So I've been patient, and I'm not a patient man by nature. But I'm blest if I want things to come to a head while Anthea's here cluttering up my life. So don't be so maddeningly aloof!'

He took hold of her hands, pulled her round to face him and said, 'Juliana, am I rushing you too much? Is this place so much at the ends of the earth, at the very back of beyond, that you feel you'll be too far from your family? I can see how close you are—that pact of thinking of each other every day at a given time makes me realise that. But in any case you're going to be scattered. Robert will take up work in India, Liesel is going to Switzerland, your parents are forever travelling ... and they'd love this place, surely? They'd often come. Why, you said your father was even born in New Zealand. He'd love climbing round here. Evidently he left it at an early age so hadn't the chance. It'd thrill him. Climbers come here from all over the world, why not Fergus Hendrie? Now look what you've made me do!' He laughed. 'I was trying to wait till we got rid of Anthea ... I'd back her to spoil anything, but I've jumped the gun. But tell me, darling, reassure me that when Anthea goes ... that you and I can ...'

She put a hand against his lips, checking his words, and he saw with amazement that her eyes were full of unshed tears. 'Thor, please! Yes, you are going too quickly. But—but even when Anthea is gone, this— Thor's Hill—can't be my world, ever. There are all sorts of reasons against it. I don't want to go into them now. Please don't ask me. This is just an attraction born of my being the only free woman in scores of miles, the fact that I love the mountains, that my father is a mountaineer ... that everyone is matchmaking ... Grizel, George, Barbara, even Willocks ... I'm here only temporarily. I know that as George was only allowed up here because of me, I must stay till the worst of the weather is over, till the time for flooded rivers and deep snows is past, but as soon as spring comes I must be on my way home. Come March I must be flying back, and I've a lot of New Zealand to see yet. I haven't even set foot on the North Island yet.'

The mist swirled around the jeep and shut them into a world of their own. Thor's face was carved in granite and the tawny eyes bored into the green. 'Something's happened,' he said abruptly but not harshly. 'You've changed. What is it? Come on, tell me. Ever since the world began women have left home and parents to be with their men, and you of all people shouldn't cling to the known and familiar, since as a family, you've always explored! Your parents belong to the world, not just to one little corner of Scotland.' He gave her a little shake, 'Come on, what is it? It's got to be Anthea. Don't I just know it! She's made mischief. Talk about the follies of youth following us and catching up with us! Just because as a half-baked youth I had no discrimination and fell for a beautiful face with nothing behind it, someone selfish to the core, malicious and a liar to boot, now it's interfering in my pursuit of the woman I've recognised as my true mate. What *has* Anthea said to you, Juliana? There's got to be something.'

The eyes that looked into his were completely honest, clear and convincing. 'Thor, in fairness to her, you've got to believe this. I know she's a mischief-maker, a disruptive influence here, *but she has made no mischeie.*'

A deep line etched itself between his brows. 'I think I've got to believe that. I think if she'd said anything to make you doubt me, a half-truth or a deliberate lie, you'd ask me for the true version. But there's some barrier now, isn't there? Something that didn't exist that night at the foot of the terrace ... or even at the Murrays' the other night. Won't you tell me? Is it something to do with Marcus? We know so little of each other's lives prior to meeting. Is it?'

Juliana gave him the same frank look. 'Thor, I've as much feeling left for Marcus as you have for Anthea, and nothing that happened in our association, anyway, could affect our—our——'

'Our relationship,' he filled in for her.

She nodded, gratefully. 'You'll just have to accept that for reasons I can't name, this homestead in the Alps is not for me. Oh, please, please understand and accept!'

The craggy lines and planes of his face softened suddenly, and to her surprise he even smiled, 'Oh, Juliana, you're kicking against the pricks, against the inevitable, and I can't think why. Leave it. I can't and won't believe it's all over between us before it's scarcely begun. Anthea may not have caused this, but I stake my oath that whatever's bothering you will dissolve like this morning mist once she's gone. I've no arguments to use against this mulish reserve of yours—so unnatural to you, I think, except this, my only weapon, which is pretty potent . . .'

The next moment he had her hard against him in the narrow confines of the jeep, and he was kissing her with a sense of possession that was indeed potent, something that almost swept away every strong feeling of the minutes before, the conviction that because this was where her father had been accused of being a thief, she could never belong.

He took his mouth from hers but kept his gaze intently upon her. 'You're fighting something you *can't* fight, Juliana Hendrie. We belong. It's as simple as that. Now be a good girl and run along to learn all you can about managing a schoolroom. You're going to need that skill—we aren't sending our children to boarding school!'

She was speechless, partly because of her tumult of feelings, partly because Thor could take her refusal of him in this way. He should have been furious. But sooner or later he was going to have to accept it.

The winds continued to rage about the Alps. They were lucky the power wasn't cut. Thor expected it hourly. He filled every lamp in the storeroom, plus the ones in the main rooms that were on pulleys. He had Juliana working with him every moment she could, determined, she guessed, to keep her away from Anthea as much as possible. They cleared culverts, an essential task with rain forming cascades down the mountainsides and bowling great boulders into the drains. Then one morning when the wind dropped and the rain ceased, into the strange stillness came the frightening but distant roar of avalanches from the water-loosened snows. In the gorge much of it fell straight into the river, damming it at intervals, then releasing it in horrifying torrents, swelling the river still more.

Deer, chamois and thar began encroaching on the grazing nearer the homestead and the whole area looked drowned and desolate. Anthea's comments were perhaps justified but hardly tactful. One night when

Juliana had slipped out to make some coffee and take it to George and Grizel who were playing backgammon in his room, she came back to hear Anthea saying to Thor, 'And even when it's like this, Tulloch, do you never yearn for a property nearer the coast? Even just on the downs?'

'No. This is in my blood, part of me.'

Anthea saw Juliana coming and said no more. Juliana felt a tide of gladness rising within her. Even if she herself could never make her home here because she would not bring that misery to her father, she was glad, glad, glad Thor would not be moved in his loyalty. Some day she would be just a memory in this man's mind, and she hoped, or told herself she hoped, he would meet a woman from near here, to share his life.

The radio news was bad—rivers up everywhere, from North Canterbury to the Far South. Now snow was predicted and farmers urged to move stock, motorists to take care and that chains would be needed even on roads close to the cities as what was sweeping up from the south was a storm of some magnitude. It was expected in the Mackenzie Country by late afternoon tomorrow.

Thor's comment was unexpected. 'It will be even worse for the farms close to the coast—they'll be lambing. Up here, of course, we don't start till the first of November. Though it'll be bad enough. We'll be out early tomorrow feeding-out, moving what we can. The sheep will sense it and be on the move down. I could wish I hadn't moved the wethers.' He looked across at Anthea. 'You sure picked a good time to drop in. I don't know when I'll get you out now.'

She said bitterly, 'I've nothing to go back to, so what does it matter?'

Juliana's throat constricted. For once she felt sorry for her. No doubt she was reaping as she had sowed, but it must be devastating to be caught in this limbo between one life and the next—whatever that next might hold. Evidently Anthea's life in Auckland was over. She'd been desperate and had turned back to where, in earlier years, she had known a caring, then found it no longer existed. Even as Juliana thought this, Anthea stood up. 'I'm going to bed. Goodnight.'

Juliana couldn't help it. 'Would you like me to bring you some chicken sandwiches and a pot of tea?' she asked.

It looked as if Anthea would refuse, but the words of proud rejection died on her lips and she said tonelessly, 'Thanks. That would be lovely.' At the door she added, 'If you're not too tired.'

Juliana and Thor were left looking at each other speculatively. He made a helpless gesture. 'Impossible not to feel sorry for her, but what can we do? I don't think she has enough reserves in herself to create a new life, take up new interests.'

Juliana said, eyes a-shine, 'Oh, Thor, I'm glad you feel like that. I didn't want you to be too hard, too unforgiving.'

'It wasn't that, Juliana. I was just plain terrified of the havoc she might cause between you and me.' His voice went dry, 'But it didn't take Anthea to do it, did it? You seem to think our lives don't lie together. Not that I'm giving up.'

Juliana got up quickly and went out to the work-kitchen to make the sandwiches. She took the tray in to Anthea. Those hard lines about her face seemed softened, and for the first time Juliana thought she looked wistful. She looked up at Juliana and said, 'Thanks, this ... thoughtful gesture means a lot to me, tonight.'

On an impulse Juliana said, sitting down on a lambskin-covered stool by the bed, 'Why particularly tonight? Would it help to talk about it? Or would you prefer just tea, not sympathy?'

Anthea didn't recoil, but said desolately, 'It's Cosmo's birthday today. I wonder how he spent it.' She knew she'd given Juliana a surprise and added defensively, 'I'm not entirely devoid of feelings. Cosmo's a big tough business man, but he sets great store on birthdays and Christmases. Just like a little boy.'

Juliana couldn't help it. She took the cup and saucer

from the exquisitely manicured hand that was trembling and said simply, 'You still care, don't you?'

Anthea put her hands up to cover her eyes. 'Much too late I know I do. We said such things to each other—irrevocable things. He despises me.'

Juliana said swiftly, 'Perhaps you only think that. My parents have a great thing going for them ... but even Mother said once that every woman and man ought to realise that a good marriage can still hold in it, at times, something of the love-hate relationship. But the love is stronger, balances it out. Perhaps, even if the divorce is near, you could make an overture ... if it doesn't come off, only your pride would take a knock.'

Anthea said, 'It was to save my pride, to save my face that I came here. When Cosmo said to me that if you didn't find your ideal you were apt to go on searching, and that he found more understanding in his secretary than in me, I couldn't take it. I thought if he knew I'd gone running off to my first love, it might bring him to his senses. But he doesn't care. I filled in three weeks at the Hermitage, thinking he'd guess I was looking for Tulloch, and he'd come after me. But he didn't. I've lost him.'

Juliana boggled. 'But what about the divorce? I mean, that takes time. This sounds a more recent parting.'

Anthea cast her eyes down. 'That's one of the reasons why Cosmo despises me. I twist the truth—there, I've admitted it. I never have before. If I'm driven into a corner I lie. I got desperate when Cosmo didn't come. I thought if I could write to him from Thor's Hill, it would stir him on. But I knew Tulloch would have nothing to do with me if he thought I'd just run off in a tiff, so I made it sound irrevocable, that a divorce was nearly through. But he wouldn't play ball anyway. He despises me too. I thought I'd just have to crook my little finger and he'd come running. Nothing's like it used to be.'

Juliana said slowly, 'I don't think you'd want it to be. It sounds to me as if Cosmo's your man.'

'He was. But not any more. He's had me.'

Juliana's voice was crisp, impatient. 'Well, you certainly give up easily! You ought to be fighting tooth and nail to get him back. This secretary was probably just a sympathetic ear, a sort of listening-post. If Cosmo despises you because you twist the truth, because you like lots of admiration, mightn't he admire you for coming to terms with it? For admitting you do ... or rather that you *did*, but intend to cut that out in the future. Instead of trying to make him jealous by appearing as if you'd fled to Tulloch, tell him you thought you'd try it on because you loved him so much. Why don't you ring him? We may be cut off in every other way, but so far the telephone wires are intact. And listen, if he's out, don't jump to the conclusion that he's out with that secretary. He could simply have gone off to a show alone to cheer himself up. Now, drink up that tea to help compose yourself and come along to the office. It's more private.'

A gleam shot into the beautiful dark eyes and a flake of colour stained the creamy matt-surface cheeks. 'I believe I will.'

'Of course you will.'

Anthea drank the tea, even nibbled half the biscuit, then thrust her feet into feathery mules, donned the turquoise négligé Tulloch had been so scathing about the other night and said, with an appealing look, 'Would you get me the number, please, Juliana? I just couldn't stand it if Cosmo hung up on me. I wouldn't blame him if he did, though.'

This augured well, Juliana thought. Oh, why was he a thousand miles away, separated by half the South Island, all the length of the North Island, and the raging Cook Strait between, with, if the predictions were right, half the airports in the country closed tomorrow? And even if they'd been open, he'd still be separated from his wife by a river called Rubicon!

Would Anthea's tones, as they were now, carry conviction, or would the memory of bitter words, words that twisted the truth, be so seared into his soul that he wouldn't listen?

'I'll get through to him,' she said. 'Would you allow

me to say who I am and that you've been staying with us and would like so much to speak to him?'

'Oh, if you would! I somehow think he'd listen to you. You'll sound so sincere. You always do. You mean you'll—you'll hint that you're Tulloch's girl?'

'I'll even say I'm already his fiancée if that'll make him speak to you,' promised Juliana recklessly. Then she laughed. 'Sounds as if I'm not above twisting the truth myself!'

She sat Anthea down in the office, excused herself, and sped to Thor, who was reading now. He looked up. 'What are you so sparkling-eyed about? I was thinking you were probably having to listen to Anthea making some double-edged remark.'

'No,' her eyes lit up even more. 'There's no divorce on the cards. She left him only a month ago. She sees herself as greatly at fault, and wants to admit it to him. She's going to ring him. I wanted to make sure you didn't burst into the office to see what was happening and to ask you would it be all right to make the call charged to here, not reversed. I want to explain to him first, and it would be ghastly if he was still so angry that if the operator asked: "Would you accept a call from Mrs Rosenby?" he answered "No." She's terrified he'll hang up on her.'

Thor looked astounded. 'Well, I'm beggared! Girl, you must be a witch. Of course have it charged to us. It's worth ringing the North Pole to get her out of our hair. But I don't like the idea of you being the chopping-block between them. Look, could I—Oh, no, I couldn't. He'd probably have an apoplexy if her ex-fiancé rang.' He came to her, touched her fingertips, said, 'What a lass . . . maid of the mountains . . . and as courageous as they come!'

'Don't . . . you'll undermine my courage. But I've got to do it,' and she was gone.

She got the number, heard it ringing, prayed Cosmo would be home, then heard the receiver lifted. The operator on the local exchange asked if that was the Auckland number and, to her dismay, a woman said it was. A young, attractive voice. Oh no, not the secretary, 'Please, dear God, don't let it be the secretary.'

She said crisply, 'May I speak to Mr Cosmo Rosenby, please?'

The girl's voice replied, 'I'm sorry, but he's not here.'

Juliana gave a tiny shake of her head at Anthea and said, 'When will he be available, please? I'm ringing from the South Island and it's important.'

'I'm so sorry, he won't be in. He's away on holiday, on a cruise. He's taking a long time off from the pressure of business. Best way of doing it, isn't it? Above all worry levels. My husband is one of his new sales representatives and we're house-hunting, so Mr Rosenby kindly let us have his house—said we could have it for at least six weeks. Does this help you any?'

Help them? How ironic! Juliana knew she mustn't sound too dismayed, rumours could fly in business circles. She said, 'Thank you. Yes, you've been most helpful. That puts us in the picture. We'll contact his manager in the morning.'

She put the phone down, said dully, 'Cosmo's on a cruise, and isn't expected back for six weeks. He's let a new employee have the house till they got their own. She said the cruise was to give him a spell from business worries. Sorry, Anthea.'

'Business worries!' said Anthea bitterly. 'To get him away from matrimonial worries, from a temperamental wife who wouldn't pull her weight. A cruise! Lots of widows go on cruises. It would serve me right if he met someone else. It could so easily happen.'

Juliana knew that was true. She put her head in her hands, then said, 'Surely to goodness he wouldn't cut himself off entirely from business? Look, there are such things as radio-telegraphs to reach ships at sea. Cosmo's manager will know where to contact him, that's for sure. We'll have to leave it till morning. You wouldn't want to ring him at home, his wife might wonder and gossip. I'll ring in the morning, ask the name of the ship—it's probably on a Pacific cruise, so it might even be in one of the island ports. In fact we could get the itinerary of it from the shipping office. You needn't give too much away, just say you'd lost it. Then wire the ship at the next port of call—more private than a radiotelegram. Telegrams are often couched in affectionate terms. You could make your address The Hermitage, and say something like: "Missing you very much stop do wish I was with you stop looking forward to your return stop I'll be in Auckland to meet you love Anthea." I'm sure he'll be missing you just as much and will read between the lines.'

Anthea lifted her head, fixed her eyes on Juliana's with a pathetic intensity and said, 'I believe that would do the trick. But oh, however am I going to wait six weeks?'

Juliana said almost gaily, 'That'll make the reunion even sweeter when it comes. Look, I said something to Tulloch. He won't make you feel embarrassed. So——'

It was the first time Anthea had shown a bit of humour. 'For sure he'll not be embarrassed. He'll be relieved. He was hating me because of you. Don't let my capers spoil anything for you, Julie. For anything that's going for you and Tulloch. I've been a bitch—no other word for it. Now, what were you going to suggest?'

'That we tell him what's happened. He won't say serve you right. If he did I'd blast his ears off. He may have some better idea of tracing Cosmo. Come on!'

Thor asked, 'How did you get on? Everything all right? I'm no end glad that——' he stopped, because Juliana had shaken her head.

She explained the situation. He muttered, 'Oh, hell! And now——?'

Juliana said, 'How long before the river subsides and the grader comes up? Because if Cosmo reacts the way I'm sure he will, Thor, he could fly back to New Zealand from the next port, and the Hermitage is much more accessible than this place. He could go straight there.' She added, 'Anyway, with a reconciliation you wouldn't want the place cluttered with ex-boy-friends.' She was striving for a lighter touch.

Thor's face was grim. He said heavily, 'Sorry . . . I've just been outside. The rain's abated, but it's snowing thickly. By the look of it, it's been falling for some time. What foul timing!'

CHAPTER EIGHT

JULIANA hadn't realised then why Thor had said just
that. She thought he meant that if Cosmo did come, it
might be harder still to get into the station, or out of it.
She also thought it quite sensible when he said he
thought they ought to ring the manager there and then
and risk any gossip. 'He's almost bound to know you're
away, Anthea, in any case.' So they did, but luck wasn't
with them. There was no answer. Perhaps he was away
temporarily.

Juliana as well as Anthea had lain awake for hours,
finding the very silence of the falling snow frightening
after the howling gales earlier. A happening like this
was common every winter, but this time grave personal
issues were at stake. That blanketing of snow seemed to
be stifling all their puny efforts at communication.

Juliana kept going over that last hour, when, between
trying the manager's number over and over, they'd
talked, all three. Anthea had caught Juliana trying to
conceal tears and had exclaimed, 'You're crying for *me*!
And I did all I could to threaten your own happiness
with Tulloch. This serves me right. I've always tried to
manipulate a situation to my own advantage, but I
can't do anything about the elements—they've beaten
me.'

Tulloch had looked at her in a way that made Juliana
glad, and proud of him. The ice and antagonism he'd
shown to Anthea was melting. He said, 'Don't despair,
Anthea. I've a feeling that your change of heart can't go
for nothing. It can't come too late. You must believe
that Cosmo has gone off on this cruise only because
he's missing you like hell, can't stand the empty house,
and is trying to take his mind off it. When he gets back
he may have only one desire, and that's to find you.'

The numbness hadn't left that lovely face. 'I'd like to
think so, but it's hardly likely. But I'll try. Even if he

never wants to live with me again I want him to know I'm sorry. Don't worry about me, you two. I'll do all I can tomorrow to contact the ship myself. It may take time, but I've got plenty of that. Your hands will be full trying to rescue buried sheep. I know because I was up here once when you were snow-raking. I was appalled, but Juliana's got what it takes.

'I won't expect him to cut short his cruise. I only want him to know I still love him despite what I said. Isn't it strange how we take the telephone for granted, but now I look on it as the one link left to me? The river's up, the ground's buried in snow, but I can still lift a receiver and—please God—miraculously become in touch with a ship calling at tropical islands.'

On that note they'd gone to bed, Thor and Juliana to the passage on the opposite side of the house to Anthea's room. As one they had paused at the door of Juliana's room, whispering. Juliana tilted her chin to look searchingly into his eyes. 'Thor, you look worried. Don't you think there's hope of a reconciliation?'

'No, it's not that. Though no one could predict how a man married to Anthea would react. Heaven only knows what he's gone through. I couldn't dash any hopes she has ... but the link she spoke of, the telephone, it could be gone by morning. Think of that weight of snow on those frail lines. In fact by daylight we could be back to the early conditions up here. We may not even have power.'

He looked down on her and smiled. 'But don't lie awake suffering for Anthea. She tried—several times when talking to me—to make mischief between us ... and failed. I know you aren't ready yet to make up your mind, but you will. Yes, you will. We're like the two halves of that scallop shell George has on his mantelpiece. We belong together. I can wait. You can mark time till you're ready. You can't get away. Your duty to George holds you here while winter storms last. Come spring you'll *know*. The dottrells will build their nests among the stones of the riverbed when the waters have subsided, the shining cuckoo will wing its way back from the Solomons, and you won't know the

garden ... the daffodil spears are first, breaking
through ice-hard ground ... and there'll be gentians
blue as any on your Swiss mountainsides. And every
tree will put on what some poet once called a garment
of joy. And you'll know you belong. Anthea, poor
Anthea, will be gone, no longer a threat to my peace of
mind.' He bent and kissed her, his hands warm about
her cheeks. Just a tender kiss, not seeking or possessive.
A caring kiss, the kiss of a man who was very sure of
himself.

Juliana had gone into her room, shut her door and
leaned against it, the tears coursing down her cheeks.
Thor's words were echoing in her ears. 'She tried to
make mischief and failed.' But she didn't fail, Thor
MacNair, she succeeded without trying. All unaware
she told me why my father left here all those years ago.
And that's the reason I dare not link my life with yours.
I couldn't deal my father a blow like that, bring him
back to the one place on earth he wanted to forget!

No wonder she hadn't slept well.

Next morning when she woke, she sprang out, pulled
the curtains back, to let in the eerie light of a landscape
blanched and cold. Moisture streamed down the
windows. Juliana went swiftly to her light switch, pulled
it down and the room was instantly flooded with a
golden glow. She heard George call out, snatched up
her blue woollen dressing-gown, tied it round her and
went in to him.

'That's one blessing left to us,' he said, smiling at her
from his pillows. 'I wish I was twenty years younger so
I could still pit my strength against the elements, rescue
the sheep from a living death. If you can get to them in
time you can save so many. Their breath melts a little
air-chamber round them and funnels a hole up through
the snow, revealing their whereabouts if it isn't too
deep. Then we snow-rake for them. But so often they
shelter under overhanging banks and if the thaw sets in
too soon they can get swept down the mountainside
into the rivers.'

Juliana took one of his gnarled old hands in hers and

said, 'George, you won't be tempted to do anything foolhardy, will you, like feeding out near the house, if we're further away? Because if you do, Thor might think that but for me, you'd have convalesced in Fairlie.'

George twinkled. 'I'll not let you down, lass. Where were you thinking you'd be?'

'You know. Like your Polly I'll be out snow-raking with the men.'

'Aye, I knew it. And Thor won't let you come to harm, and the more you're with him the better, not cooped up with that poisonous woman we're landed with.'

Juliana said, 'Listen, George—and you can tell Grizel. This is what happened last night.' She told him all.

George's brow cleared. 'I'd never have believed it! Well, here's hoping she can trace him and they can get together somewhere away from Thor's Hill. I want nothing to come between——'

'George! You mustn't. I know it seems as if the two of us——' She broke off, said helplessly, 'Everyone's got carried away by the knowledge that I'm Fergus Hendrie's daughter, so it seems as——'

He grinned unrepentantly, 'No seeming about it. The fact that you're Hendrie's daughter is just a bonus. You were meant for each other. But I'm a clumsy old beggar, I'm jumping the gun. Oh, aye, I'll leave the pair of you alone.'

'That's better. I must fly. It'll be all hands on deck today.'

She had a sketchy wash instead of a shower. Tubbing would be necessary tonight after a day in the snow. Her eyes met her mirrored eyes and shrank from the knowledge in them, the yearning. No, it wasn't a bonus being Hendrie's daughter, it was an insuperable barrier to happiness. Meanwhile, Juliana, take the days as they come, working side by side with the man you love ... something to remember when you're back on the other side of the world.

She came into the kitchen to see Thor replacing the

receiver of the telephone, and the fact that it gave no terminating tinkle as usual struck a blow to her heart for Anthea.

'Thor! It's out?'

'Afraid so. Dead as a doornail. I tried to raise Dragonshill and Craigievar in case our connecting lines there were still on, because then I could have given them a message to say when it's possible I'd like a helicopter in to take hay and men to further-out sheep. However, that's out. They'll survive a few days and we can save a good many of the nearer ones. But the chopper's a terrific help. However, with these white-outs over the peaks it wouldn't be possible yet. But if they could get in, they could take Anthea out. From the Mount Cook Village she'd have a much better chance of contacting Cosmo.' His eyes lit up as he noticed her outfit. 'You're prepared to come out with me?'

Juliana nodded. 'George told us such yarns in hospital about his Polly under such circumstances, I've a yen to try it. That's one experience of the snows, I've not had.'

'Good girl!' He flicked her glowing cheek with one finger. 'I'll start the breakfast if you hop along and tell Anthea the bad news about the phone.' He grinned, 'I'm not going into her bedroom for anything! I felt sorry for her last night, but I'm still pretty wary. I know her moods, and she can act like a spoilt child. I don't want her taking it out on you, through me.'

'She won't this time,' said Juliana, eyes shining. 'I just know it.'

Thor said, 'Don't look like that . . . all lit up. When you look like that I want everything between us cut and dried. I can understand now the caveman of old dragging their women off by the hair.'

She couldn't help it, she burst out laughing and departed.

Her mood stilled before she reached Anthea's room, though. How terrible for a runaway wife, longing for a reconciliation, cooped up in a pocket of the mountains, isolated by the forces of nature, tortured by the knowledge that a husband, perhaps driven reckless by her behaviour, was visiting the paradises of the South Pacific, in possibly glamorous company.

Anthea was lying looking into space; Juliana's face gave her away. Anthea raised herself up and said, 'We're cut off? The line's gone?'

Juliana nodded and her eyes filled with tears. Anthea looked at her and said quietly, 'Right, I can take it . . . this is to teach me something. I only hope I've not made shipwreck entirely of Cosmo's life as well as my own.'

Juliana's eyes betrayed admiration then. 'Oh, Anthea, that's the right way to take it, to think of him before yourself. Look, I know it's going to be an ordeal waiting for the phone to be restored, but I'd be awfully glad if you'd lend Grizel a hand. It's such a big house and I think even Willocks will be out with the rescue team, so we'll be feeding the men too, and I want to be out snow-raking.'

Anthea threw a leg out of bed. 'I will, and if there's anything I can do outside I will. I was up here in conditions like this once and have some idea. I'm sure I'll be capable of digging out paths to the fowl-houses and feeding them, for a start. I'll be with you in a jiffy.'

It was a gruelling day, yet rewarding. Juliana was surprised at the philosophical way the men took it. That spoke of years of such happenings. They were prepared for everything they found. Thor had even said as they first fared forth, 'It's so beautiful . . . despite being so treacherous.' The sloping land about the homestead had many dips and hollows, of course, but now they were filled in as if planed smooth by a master hand and in some of the lower land, not even a top strand of the barbed wire fences could be seen. It was quite evident they would be going out on skis, or snowshoes.

The others waved them off and they sped across to join Don and the other men. Barbara was regretful that she couldn't accompany them, but she and Jemmie were already busy with shovels, clearing paths and feeding the goats the children were rearing for house-milk, and Marian and Todd were raring to be off with the men and dogs. Jemmie said stoutly, 'Next year I'll be off

with the men, tramping out tracks for the sheep, but
this is—um—essential work too.'

'It sure is,' said Thor. 'I can't think of anything worse
after a bad day on the hill than coming back here to
shovel snow. You're on the payroll from this minute,
Jemmie.'

The mountains were an awesome sight, so thickly
blanketed about their lower shoulders and ridges,
usually so jagged and featured that there was a
sameness about them, because the gullies were filled.
The tops were hidden in a great mass of cloud and
white-outs that meant it was still snowing thickly up
there.

Suddenly a watery sun broke through, in the east,
occasioning a cheer from the men. Some of the steeper
places hadn't quite such a thick covering, and tramping
a path to these was more rewarding. Once heaved out
of their igloo-like drifts, the sheep were able to scramble
to these places where thawing would occur soonest, and
once some tussock was bared, they were content.

It was back-breaking, slogging work and it seemed
incredible such numbers could be saved by this small
bunch of people in comparison to the tally of ewes,
hoggets, wethers, but grim determination and fortitude
paid dividends. Even the knowledge of how short the
winter day was up there didn't force them into making
the mistake of rushing too much, for this wasn't
something to be done in a valiant spurt, but would take
days. If only the snow didn't come near the homestead
again, if it kept to the tops, they could save so many.

They had to hand it to Anthea. Her fretting,
unbearable longing to be in touch with Cosmo she kept
to herself, gritted her teeth and won the respect of not
only Thor and Juliana who had seen her at her lowest,
but also of George and Grizel, and, most surprising of
all, Barbara.

She'd helped them make pots of soup, casseroles,
steamed puddings, for appetites that were enormous;
kept the paths free over and over again from the
seeping moisture from the banked-up snow on each
side, moisture that turned to ice so quickly in these

temperatures; she made the hens and cocks steaming hot mash, even replenished the kerosene lamps in their quarters under George's supervision in the storeroom, so they could be hung up to prevent the birds freezing to their perches as had been known some years back.

The power held for two days, surprisingly, then at four on the second day, they came back to find the house lamplit. Juliana thought it very cosy that night with the warm glow from mantelpiece and table, and a big one on a pulley in the centre. Their useless electric lights were each side of it. The wood fire was glowing at one end, at the other the diesel range purred and roared.

Juliana looked across at Thor, sunk in the depths of a huge armchair, his legs sprawled out in utter weariness as they listened to their battery radio . . . and a wave of love for him swept her with such an intensity that it was also physical. Oh, God, wasn't there some way out of this? she thought. Why did she have to fall in love here, in the one place that was for her a forbidden Eden? At that moment Thor looked up and at her as she sat at the table, attaching a steel buckle to her ski-trousers. Neither of them smiled, just looked, and fleetingly that look isolated them in a world of their own. When he looked away her bright resolution wavered for a moment. *Could* she turn her back on all this? She didn't know.

The local news finished with its horrifying tale of sheep losses, its report that the far high-country stations were cut off and without power or telephone, news of roads being blocked, warnings from the traffic department to respect the conditions, and as it ended Thor almost turned it off, then said, 'Oh, we'd better listen to the rest of the world. I always appreciate this programme, *Farther Afield*. We can't be too insular . . . too wrapped up in ourselves.'

Some of it wasn't too pleasant, always some coup, mainly bloody, acts of violence on the world scene, disturbing reports of the drug traffic, all making them feel their battle with natural hazards was not the worst of all conflicts. Then, relief from the grimness ... a report, the announcer said, on aid to Nepal. 'Returning to base last Thursday, with their party, were Fergus and Astrid Hendrie. Here is our interview with them.'

The five people listening sat bolt upright, and concentrated, as Fergus Hendrie's voice came from the great continent to his daughter, snowbound among heights similar to those among which he dwelt. Juliana, her sister and brother, had often had this experience, hearing their father's voice speaking to them from other lands, but never had it been so poignant. Fergus spoke of the Nepalese so affectionately, so admiringly. 'They're so stoical, have such integrity, such qualities of friendship.' Then came her mother's voice, with its faint hint of a foreign accent. It was almost too much for Juliana.

When it was done Thor said, 'Thank heaven I didn't switch off! Juliana, we've got to get them here. I'm sure they could make it.'

She didn't know how white her face had become. She said quietly, 'I think their movements are mapped out for weeks ahead. It just isn't possible, Thor.'

George said, 'Well, let's hope for a cancellation in their engagements. We'll get in touch with them to let them know that if there's any chance at all we'd love to have them stay here. You'll have an address to reach them, Juliana? Tell them Edmund Hillary did some of his early climbing round Dragonshill and Lilybank. No harm done if they can't come, but they ought to have the opportunity. I've read his books for years, I'd sure like the privilege of having him under my roof.'

Later Thor said, 'You heard that bit on the local news about them getting hay in by helicopter to some of the stations in the Mackenzie? I sure wish we had the phone back, I'd get them in. It would be worth whatever it costs. We'd reach the distant sheep in time then. And if we had the phone, Anthea, you could start trying to contact Cosmo.'

She said quickly, 'I've resigned myself to waiting. It's bound to be re-connected before too long. Perhaps this is to teach me patience, something I've never had. All my life I've wanted what I've wanted, immediately. This time I've got to wait.'

By the fourth night they were tired to the point of exhaustion. They decided to retire early. The radio news had been better, no more snow expected except for a few isolated falls, and it said power and phones were being restored rapidly throughout the South Island, though the outlying stations could expect privation in this regard a little time yet.

Anthea took a couple of aspirins and retired early. They'd come back today to find she'd sawed up a vast quantity of frozen meat for the dogs, to thaw it quickly, a job none of them relished after a big day on the hill. Her arms were aching intolerably, and she fell asleep without even blowing her candle out. Juliana tiptoed in and saw to it. They'd all showered and changed in daylight, but Thor, after his bedtime snack, said, 'I'm taking this lamp into the bathroom. I'm going to have a good soak. My muscles are crying out for hot water.'

Juliana nodded, 'Nothing like it, but you'll be careful with the lamp, won't you? And for goodness' sake don't fall asleep in the bath. After a day like this you could, easily.'

'I'll be careful, don't lie awake wondering about the lamp . . . or me.'

She said sturdily, 'I wouldn't go to sleep leaving anyone as exhausted as you in a tub of water deep enough to ease pulled muscles. I'll read till you come out. Will it be all right if I take this lamp into the office? It's nearer the bathroom, and I can tap on the door if I think you've dropped off.'

'Okay, I'll put the lamp in a safe place for you.' He set it down on the long built-in desk, cleared a space for her book. He paused at the door and said over his shoulder, 'I like you caring about me.'

Juliana jumped like a startled fawn when the telephone gave its strident ring right at her elbow. She snatched it up before it could waken Grizel or George, or get Thor leaping out of his bath. She said quickly, 'Thor's Hill Station here . . . this is our first ring for days, who is it, please?'

The next moment she almost collapsed as a very pleasantly timbred voice said, 'Cosmo Rosenby here, though you may never have heard of me. May I know to whom I'm speaking?'

'I'm Juliana Hendrie. Oh, Cosmo, I certainly have heard of you, and how glad I am to hear you! Tell me, is this a very long-distance call? I mean are you speaking from some port in the Pacific?'

'In the Pacific? What gave you that idea? I'm at the Hermitage—got in just before the road was cut and have been trying to get you ever since. Can you tell me if my wife happens to be there?'

Juliana closed her eyes against the surprise, the relief of it. 'She most certainly is, and just longing to see you. She——'

His voice was like the crack of a pistol. *'What?'*

She said very quickly, 'Cosmo, let me explain. Before we go any further, let me explain.' A sound in the doorway made her look up. Thor was there, a dressing-gown clutched round him, dripping soapy water all over the office carpet. She said into the mouthpiece, 'Just a moment, will you?' and covered it with her hand. Thor was mouthing 'Cosmo?' at her.

She said, 'It's him, he's at the Hermitage. Hold everything till I get something out.

'Are you there, Cosmo? Sorry about that. Thor . . . that is, Mr Tulloch MacNair has just arrived in, excited of course about being connected again. So——'

The voice went grim, 'Oh, yes, Mr Tulloch MacNair. The man my wife fled to when we had a disagreement. Well, let——'

Juliana said desperately, 'Cosmo, it—it wasn't quite like that. She did rush up here, yes. But——' temptation yawned before her . . . after all, Thor had fobbed Anthea off with such a suggestion, and it had worked . . . now perhaps she could save the situation with it . . . it was even more dicey than before so why not? She said firmly, 'Cosmo, before you say another word I should tell you I'm Juliana Hendrie and I'm engaged to Tulloch. Anthea simply came up here because she was miserable, and stayed at the Hermitage to try to get hold of herself, thinking she could think things out. And she has—oh, believe me she has. While she was there, she got a chance of a lift up in a light plane, just for a few hours. She thought it would fill in time for her, but they couldn't take her back, got a call to another place, and then the river rose.

'I guess she left you a note, wives usually do, and perhaps said she was running off to Tulloch. Just the sort of overwrought thing a wife could say if she thought she'd lost her husband to another woman, and I assure you she did think that. No, please let me get it all out. I'm terrified this line fails again.

'She's been utterly miserable about you and she's shouldering a very heavy burden of guilt. She and I have become such friends and she broke down and told us how foolishly she'd behaved. She tried to ring you the night the snow started, only we didn't know it *had* started then, and got me to get the number for her, and the woman who answered the phone said she was renting the house because you'd gone off on a cruise, for six weeks!' Juliana gulped, tried to infuse a little amusement into her voice. 'You know what we women are when we think we've lost all we care about. She got to imagining all sorts of things—moonlight on the boat deck, the glamour of coral islands and so on. We tried to ring your manager to find out which ship, and the itinerary, so we could get you by radio-telephone or at the next port of call, but he must have been out, because there was no answer. When the phone was cut off next morning Anthea was in the depths of despair. Here we are, feet deep in snow, digging out sheep from the drifts, hoping to get a helicopter in to drop hay to the faraway huts and get men ferried out to them ... and we couldn't do a thing with no phone.

'Poor Anthea, she's been beside herself, but we've had to admire her ... she's pitched right in ... dug all the paths out round the house, even had all the frozen dog-tucker sawn up for us yesterday when we got back ... yes, truly. Now, I've put you in the picture, what can we do? What did you say, Oh, Cosmo, how wonderful! I must tell Thor ... Tulloch to you. He's right here, dripping water all over the carpet because he rushed out of the bath when he heard your ring.' She didn't bother covering the mouthpiece this time, 'Thor darling, Cosmo says the Dragonshill people managed to clear the road over the bridge and reach the first station on the lake road. That phone wasn't out. They're sending helicopter services in tomorrow to all the stations they think are in dire need ... if flying conditions permit it. They're bringing Cosmo in with them and will take him and Anthea out. How's that for news?'

She came back to Cosmo. 'I'll get Anthea for you ... she was worn out and went to bed at half-past eight. Cosmo, be sweet to her, won't you?'

Cosmo's answer made her say: 'Yes, of course you will—how silly of me! Hang on.'

Thor went to the phone, said, 'Cosmo, at last we meet. I've heard you're a jolly good chap. Thank heaven you're here! Anthea's just about been going out of her mind. But she's been a brick. Honestly, I didn't know she had it in her.' He went on talking, giving Cosmo instructions for the helicopter pilot.

Juliana had picked up a torch, bent over Anthea and shook her gently awake. 'Come on, Anthea ... come on, darling. Wake up, we're on the phone again. And guess who's on the line? Your Cosmo! No, not from the islands, from the Hermitage. Truly, love, I haven't invented it. Anthea, don't shiver ... he really is there and I've talked to him at length. Told him how you are, how you feel, how you've worked. How you were trying to contact him. Anthea, put something on ...' But it was useless, Anthea was running like the wind to get to the phone.

Juliana seized Anthea's wrap, fled after her. Anthea snatched the phone off Thor, leaving him in mid-sentence, and said, 'Cosmo!' in a tone that said it all. Juliana flung the wrap round her shoulders, clutched Thor, and they went off to the kitchen.

There wasn't a light left burning there, just the glow of the fires. There were no words for the gladness they felt. They found themselves in each other's arms, holding tightly together in a nameless ecstasy of delight. He kept on kissing her. Then Juliana pushed him away a little and said in a tone of reproof, 'You mustn't have dried yourself at all—that dressing-down is soaking! I'll get you George's.' She darted off, filched it from the foot of George's bed, returned, and handed it to him.

He raised a quizzical brow. 'I'm waiting,' he said pointedly. 'I know you've been nursing for years, but it could looked decidedly odd if Grizel or Anthea came in . . . though even if we said we'd just got engaged, they might look askance!' His eyes were alight.

She clapped a rueful hand to her mouth. 'I'd forgotten I said that to Cosmo. But I had to, for Anthea's sake.'

His mouth twitched. 'I've no quarrel with it. In fact I wouldn't mind if it snowed again.'

She looked at him with incredulity. 'Oh, dear, you're getting lightheaded! Must be the relief of knowing Anthea is going. Snow is the last thing we want.'

'Dope . . . if Cosmo gets snowed in with us, you can't cast me off.'

Suddenly she was helpless with laughter. 'Thor, you idiot! Right, I'm turning my back.'

They sat down in the old rattan chairs that graced each side of the range, their feet on the rag mat. Juliana saw Thor's face settle into serious lines. 'Juliana, I've a feeling that when we get Anthea out of our hair, things between us will get into right perspective. There's so much I don't understand. I know we got off on the wrong foot—I was so against you coming up here. I soon changed my tune, didn't I? Seems incredible now. I think I was fighting an instant attraction and distrusted it because of Anthea's behaviour all those years ago. I didn't want to be vulnerable again and have another woman only agree to marry me if I moved to an easier access place.'

She didn't know how to find words. When first she met Thor she had certainly not thought of him as vulnerable. She'd thought him rock-hard, flint-sharp, unyielding, but now she knew him only too well. He'd been what when he first met Anthea? Twenty-four? And still raw from losing his parents so tragically.

No doubt he'd dreamed of Anthea having a nature to match her undoubted beauty, but instead she'd shown herself as selfish, abominably demanding, imperious, cruel. So he hadn't wanted another woman up here, especially one fresh from London. In spite of all they had been irresistibly drawn to each other. Then he found out that she too was a child of the mountains and he was dreaming dreams again. Apart from their kindred interests, there was an alchemy between them that added up to sheer rapture, and he knew it. He would try to batter down her defences, but she must be strong. She would have to think of something, invent some valid-sounding reason as soon as possible when these immense barriers of flooded river and smothering snow were gone.

Perhaps she could secretly ring Liesel and tell her she must ring here and ask her to return home immediately. Invent a mythical aunt lying helpless and needing nursing, or something. She would persuade George it was better for him to go to the Fairlie house now, within call of a doctor. Grizel could go with him and no doubt Barbara or Willocks would cook Thor's meals. A pang shot through her. All she wanted to do was stay here, in these Delectable Mountains, to minister to all Thor's needs.

Thor said, 'What is it? One moment you were all delight, now your face has shadows chasing over it.'

She must be careful; this man was too perceptive. She proved that a moment later. When it appeared that she wouldn't, couldn't answer him he said, 'It's to do with the reason you won't marry me. Isn't it? *Isn't it?*'

She looked across at him, defencelessly, vulnerable, scared. 'Please don't, Thor. I've got to make my own decisions. I ought not to have come here—I can't tell you why. I wish I could.'

He came across, knelt on the rag rug and put a hand each side of her waist. 'But you can. You can tell *me* anything. Because we belong.—Can you mean there's some secret, something you're in honour bound not to divulge? Because it concerns someone else? It's all I can think of.'

The green eyes on a level with his regarded him honestly. 'You could say that. It's no use, Thor, no use at all.'

He ought to have lost his temper then, told her she was absurd, that it wasn't fair to a man who offered his all not to tell him why she was refusing him, but he just smiled and said, 'I could use those same words, Juliana. Because it *isn't any use*. No use you thinking I'll let you go. You can't escape me, not ever. Even if you went to the uttermost ends of the earth.'

Juliana dropped her lashes down swiftly. His grip tightened. 'Ah, I believe you've been planning just that. To leave here, return home to Scotland. Well, what matter? I've always wanted to visit Scotland again, so I would only follow you.' His expression broke up, and he chuckled, 'Think of the scandal it would cause in your village! I'd camp on your doorstep. Or up on Ben Thor, in my little bell tent, looking down on your cottage.'

'You're crazy,' she told him. 'Less than three months ago you didn't even know I existed. Life will settle down again when I'm gone.'

'I won't give it the chance. I'm serious about this.'

'You aren't. Can you think of anything more ridiculous?'

'Yes, I can. I have a most inventive brain. I could fly to India, present myself to your parents as the ideal husband for a mountaineer's daughter, and get them to fly to Scotland with me; great publicity would attend that ... the conquering heroes returning with their future son-in-law.'

She instinctively recoiled, even though it must only be fun. 'There were no peaks conquered this time. They've just been assisting with the building of a hospital. Dad organised the raising of the money in Britain.'

His eyes narrowed. 'It *is* something to do with your parents. I know it.'

Hot betraying colour rose right up from her throat.

She was dismayed and rose to her feet, saying, simulating anger, 'Who do you think you are, a thought-reader? Sir Omniscience? Please, Thor, stop it. I can hear Anthea coming—we mustn't let her think we're quarrelling.'

'We can't be quarrelling. It takes two. I'm just stating a fact. *That you are my woman and I'm not going to let you go*. Oh, Anthea, here you are . . . no need to ask is everything all right? . . . you're radiant!'

'No, no need,' said Anthea. 'Cosmo was wonderful. I—oh, it was too lovely! So much more than I deserve. He made it quite plain that the helicopter pilot said our return with them will be entirely at their convenience, the run-holders and their stock come first. That their job will take hours, they'll have to ferry men and feed out to outlying huts and possibly lift some sheep out in wool-bale slings to sunny faces . . . have I got that right? It seems incredible. And——' she suddenly dimpled and looked ten years younger, 'and he said that on no account am I to hold up any of the rescue work, that you've been unbelievably good to me and he'd like me to leave a good impression on you all at the last. And I thought he'd stopped caring!'

'You goose, Anthea,' said Juliana. 'I've always believed in happy endings.'

'Of course you have,' said Thor meaningfully, and turned to Anthea, 'and never more so than now, when her own happy ending is so near. Now, girls, it's going to be one hell of a day tomorrow—bed!'

They woke to a grey dawn, but Thor's belief that the sun would soon come through was justified. George and Grizel had been put in the picture about Cosmo and that he might get in with the helicopter. George said, 'Thank God for that, now perhaps we'll be able to get our own lives sorted out.' Thor had brought his elderly cousin in a cup of tea, and laughed, his eyes seeking Juliana's. She refused to smile back. Grizel had strolled in, to ask what was all the ringing the night before, and chuckled and said, 'Tonight I'll emulate my small grandson in Christchurch. When I was there he said his prayers to me, and they consisted mostly of "Thank You, God for motorcycles and trucks and cars and tricycles." I'll say my thanks for helicopters that can bring in hay and lift men out to the huts to rescue hundreds of buried sheep, and reunite a husband and wife in the nick of time.'

'Nick of time, Grizel?' queried Thor. 'What do you mean?'

She was quite candid. 'Before yon woman could do any lasting harm. What else would I mean?'

It seemed an age before they heard the chopper, though they used every moment just in case, packing supplies. That was the women's job and the men did all they could to have the bales of hay ready and the bags of sheep-nuts. Yesterday Don had used the front-end loader as a snow-plough and cleared great tracks around the houses and outbuildings, and the sun struggling through made them all feel better in their anxiety for the sheep further up.

Anthea looked much less like the dangerous other-woman type than she had on arrival. She was wearing a bright scarlet ski-suit of Barbara's that had seen much wear, a woollen hat Juliana had provided, with a pompon on the top. An old scarf of Thor's was wound round her throat and she was huddled into what Juliana called an Edmund Hillary coat, a sort of three-quarter waterproof in grey, with rabbitskin collar and cuffs, a real utility garment. 'I don't want Cosmo to think I'm just an ornament up here . . . as usual,' she'd said nervously.

Juliana had taken her by the shoulders and shaken her. 'Anthea, I feel you've found yourself up here. I think you're the woman now that Cosmo wants you to be. I spoke to him for such a short time last night, and it must have been terrible for him, a perfect stranger discussing his matrimonial affairs—but oh, girl, did we get down to basics! There was no restraint whatever.' She grinned. 'I couldn't stand you when you first appeared on the scene, might as well confess it, but now I feel as if I've known you for years.'

Tears threatened, but Anthea dashed them away. 'Oh, Juliana, I've never had a close woman friend. Most women detest me. I used to put it down to jealousy, and I was almost proud of it. But you're different. We mustn't lose touch. You must come and stay with us in Auckland, you and Tulloch, Cosmo asked me quite despairingly once when was I going to grow up, to stop thinking what effect my looks had on people, stop trying to attract men to make him think how lucky he was. To remember I wasn't nineteen any more. It was so stupid of me. Perhaps coming up here was the right thing to do after all. Yet even that I only did to make Cosmo jealous.'

Juliana found she could laugh over that now. 'Tell him that. If you hadn't cared for him, you wouldn't have thought of trying it on. Actually all you succeeded in doing was to make *me* jealous.'

Anthea looked stricken with conscience. 'I could have made a mess of things for you. Oh, I nearly forgot—I thought of it last night before I went to sleep. That was a straight-out lie I told you about that poem . . . about Tulloch saying Robert Herrick's poem meant he'd known an Anthea just like me. So . . . well, I've confessed. It just wasn't true.'

'What wasn't true?' Thor asked, making them jump. Juliana said quickly, 'There are some things not good for men to know. They could get above themselves. It's entirely something between two women. We understand what makes each other react, where men just wouldn't. It didn't mean a thing.'

Anthea looked up, mischief touching her eyes. 'There's no reason why she shouldn't tell you, Tulloch. I think you'd rise to the occasion and it could spark off a tender moment. Not now, but when all the shouting and tumult has died and the sheep are all rescued and you're alone together again at Thor's Hill, ask again. She was dead jealous—I saw her face. So it's a compliment to you.'

Thor stared; this was an Anthea he'd never seen. He

lifted his glasses, slung round his neck, scanned the sky that was becoming more blue every moment, concentrated on the south-west, then gave a shout, 'There it is . . . they're coming!'

Most of the Thor's Hill folk assembled on the landing-pad had seen this operation before, but also all of them could recall when the only way to reach the distant buried sheep was on foot, through the drifts. So it was still a modern miracle.

The welcome sound neared, in no time it had sunk down with a precision still to be marvelled at. Out piled the pilot, his offsider, and a third figure, tall, broad, and in gear that must have been borrowed for the occasion. A man prepared to help if needed. As they emerged, from under the whirling blades slowing down, Anthea took off and at that same moment the third figure broke into a run, and caught her up as she reached him.

Thor said in Juliana's ear, 'I think I'm going to like Cosmo. He's evidently got no inhibitions. Imagine having a grand reunion in front of an audience like this!'

Fortunately they were far enough off not to have their utterances made audible, but there wasn't much talking being done at that. The group had watched, fascinated, but now they suddenly came to life, greeted the helicopter men and talk turned on the job in hand. Questions were asked about general conditions in the province, the state of affairs in Mount Cook Village with stranded tourists, the further prospects, the happenings on the other runs.

Thor said, 'I just wish old Madame Beaudonais could have seen what a boon her dream of a bridge has been, not only to Dragonshill but to the whole of the Tekapo isolated stations. For that run to be able to get across and make contact was terrific—it's served us all. Madame is one pioneer woman who will never be forgotten as long as the mountains last and snows fall.'

CHAPTER NINE

FEVERISH activity now prevailed. Juliana was amazed at the easy way Thor greeted Cosmo. She had imagined him retreating into a dour shell. Not so. He was very much master of the situation and host to a guest. Some of it, perhaps, was as a façade in front of the men who had brought Cosmo in.

Then Thor said, with a note of pride and possession, 'This is Juliana, Cosmo . . . and after your conversation with her last night, you hardly need an introduction. Man, were we glad to have that phone ring and to have the news!'

That could have meant either of two things . . . the news that Cosmo was only a chopper flight away, instead of in the Pacific, or that succour was at hand for the trapped sheep. He added, 'I guess you'd feel really cheated if you weren't able to tell your Auckland friends you were right in the thick of the rescue operation here, so we'll take you up with us, Anthea too, and of course Juliana was coming in any case. As Fergus Hendrie's daughter she's not likely to be kept away from it.'

Reg and Bill were thunderstruck. 'Fergus Hendrie's daughter? Tulloch MacNair, how lucky can a man get? But how come we've not heard she was staying here? They'd be tickled pink to have her at the village. Why, just the other night the Hendries were on TV. They'd just got back down fron some Nepalese hospital they're interested in.'

Juliana gave a cry that revealed how much she longed to see her parents. 'Oh . . . tell me, how did they look? Did they seem well? We only heard them on the radio.'

'They looked fine. Good heavens, they don't look old enough for you to be their daughter. I expect it's the life they lead.' Bill continued: 'This is great. No doubt they'll come across here now—they're bound to. What

150

a welcome they'll get! You'll be first-class news, too, Juliana. When all this hoo-ha is over and access easier, we must put on a slap-up affair for you. Fergus Hendrie's daughter living among us! It beats the band!'

She dared not tone this down in front of Cosmo and Anthea. Cosmo had probably said something to these men about Juliana and Thor being engaged. But it filled her with apprehension. Well, there was nothing she could do about it at the moment. Not till Cosmo and Anthea were on their way back to their own home. Those two worlds might never touch again. And now, anyway, they must get on.

They piled into the helicopter, men, women, dogs, the children watching enviously, but they couldn't risk taking them where drifts could be over their heads. Nearer the homestead, they were glad to use them to help stamp out tracks for the animals.

Oh, what a magic world this was ... soaring up over such an unbelievable spread of newly-fallen snow, and all the vast panorama spread out below them ... with range upon range coming into view, and valley and gorge she hadn't known existed. Just as Dad had said in his book, the higher you go, the further you push the horizons away, the wider your views.

It was impossible not to be lost in wonder and equally impossible not to feel a little scared. Anthea put out a gloved hand to Cosmo, whose vivid blue eyes were alight like a boy's at this unexpected adventure. He tightened his grip on it. Anthea said, pitching her voice beneath the noise, 'Juliana, this will be nothing to you if you were with your parents in Nepal. I expect familiarity breeds contempt.'

In answer, she put her lips close to Anthea's ear, 'No, my father always says that the day we lose our awe of the mountains and their hazards, we're in danger.'

They came down gently on the lower slopes of the hill where the Main Slog Hut was perched. The other huts were not going to be used, as they were mustering huts, too high for sheep in winter, even if they rarely had so heavy a fall so late. It was sturdily built, of corrugated iron, with some stone, heavily wired down to immense pegs driven into the rocks to anchor it against the fearsome winds which could sweep up the valley, or hurl themselves from the tops in screaming frenzy. The dog shelters were on the lee side, just as sturdily built.

They lit the fire from the enormous stack of dry wood there, piled the provisions out, drank scalding cups of coffee straight from the flasks, set a huge black kettle filled with snow on the iron bars of the fireplace, then piled into the chopper again to spot the snow-camps where the sheep would be huddled together, landed in a likely area and the work began. The chopper flew off again with Collard and Pete on board, directing them to throw off the hay-bales and sacks of concentrates for later use.

Here was where experience and the craft of the mountain men came into full use ... they knew the lie of the land, even in the drifts that obscured the features, where the shelter points would be, where, under what looked like a uniform covering of snow, the sunniest faces would be found and could be cleared.

Then they made tracks to these for the sheep to use, when they'd been brought out, hard, gruelling, backbreaking work, forcing reluctant animals along those icy tracks to those areas. Not till they saw tussock and snowgrass sticking up, and hay being spread, did they deign to hurry along at all. It was heartening to find not too many had succumbed. Wonderful how long these animals could survive ... bringing home to them that slogan: 'There is no substitute for wool,' but there were enough of the weaker members, stiff and stark, for the dog tucker needed, all right. That would mean work back at the camp later, skinning and breaking up.

They were amazed at Cosmo. All his private worries seemed put aside, and his energies bent on helping these people who had restored his wife to him—not only restored her, but somehow had called out in her qualities he'd thought were lacking. He grinned at Juliana, helping her shove a particularly aggressive and stubborn wether along, 'Never had such an adventure in my life! I wish my board members could see me. I'll dine out on it for years. And, Juliana, thank you.'

She whispered, 'Cosmo, I did nothing. I was just a sympathetic ear when she felt so wretched and felt she'd brought it all on herself. She suddenly thought about it being your birthday ... said you made a lot of birthdays and Christmases ... and the floodgates opened. I felt so despairing when I found you were out of reach—or seemed to be. When that woman who's renting your house said your manager had told her you were on a cruise, it was so ghastly.'

'It was a face-saving excuse. I didn't want anyone to know Anthea had fled down here—it savoured of an eternal triangle. I told my manager I wanted to be free of all business worries for a few days ... and I'd get in touch with him before too long, that meanwhile he could tell business associates I was on a cruise and incommunicado. But I still want to thank you. Thank you for just being there to listen. And for being who you are. I don't mean Fergus Hendrie's daughter, I mean for being Tulloch's fiancée. When you told me that all despair fell from me. Just look at Anthea, will you? It beats all. See ... freeing that animal from snow. I've never seen her like this.' He plunged off in her direction because that wether was down, cramped and cold. He heaved it to its feet.

The sun rose higher, became warmer. The light on the snow was blinding, even with sun-glasses. Only their faces and hands were numbed at times. The vigour of the work rose body temperatures.

Thor came across, snow clinging in little tufts to his heavy brows, as tough as the mountains about him. 'We're doing fine. The losses will be much less because of the chopper—it's a great service. They've done Dragonshill and Heronscrag. This afternoon they'll take you three back to the house, but I'll have to be up here with the men, of course. Once we've got the hay lifted in, we can work it from here. It makes four of us. The chopper will go back for another lot, drop it, take you back, then take off for Craigievar. They'll stay the night there, work all day tomorrow and come back for us the next day. I'm afraid, Cosmo, you and Anthea will have to stay on. They'll get you out after that.

Nothing I can do about getting you back to the Hermitage before that. Time for the sheep on all these properties is too precious, apart from the money it costs for the hire of the helicopter.'

'Suits me very well. Best adventure of my life to date.'

'And Anthea?' asked Thor.

Cosmo grinned. 'She can't do much about it, even if she wanted to, can she? Besides, even if she could, where I am, she stays.'

'Good man! There's plenty of room at the homestead.' Thor grinned too. 'I'm afraid at first I made Anthea anything but welcome, but the pair of you together makes a very different kettle of fish.'

Juliana was horrified at this blunt speaking. She said, 'Thor!' in a tone of such reproof that Cosmo burst out laughing. 'It's all right, Juliana. I like the sound of that very much. Imagine what a fellow goes through when his wife leaves a note saying she's been unhappy and misunderstood and she's going off to the chap she fancied years ago! I waited for a bit to see if she came back. Besides, I had a lot on my plate business-wise. Then I panicked. I knew so little about you, Tulloch, that I felt anything might've happened.

'Worst of all was feeling that it was my own fault. I was so tired of Anthea wanting the admiration of every male in our orbit, I tried to pay her out in her own coin and hinted that I found more kindness and understanding in my secretary. Just as well the said secretary never knew, she'd have thought I'd gone off my rocker! It had the opposite effect from what I'd intended. It sent her flying off down here. Thank heaven you'd got yourself engaged to someone else in the interim!'

'Good show, wasn't it?' agreed Thor. The tawny eyes caught and held Juliana's. 'Mind you, if Anthea had come a month or two earlier it could have put the cat among the pigeons ... I'd only just got this wench to accept me.'

Cosmo looked swiftly at Juliana, her eyes dancing. 'It seems to be the time for being candid ... it's all right, Cosmo, I wouldn't have let anyone get him away from me. I was just playing hard to get.' She pulled a rueful face. 'And I'd no sooner accepted him than Anthea descended upon us, the river rose, then we got snowed in, and when we'll get a chance to go down country to buy my engagement ring, I don't know!'

Cosmo said, 'Oh, was that it? I noticed your left hand was ringless but thought you'd just be scared of losing it doing work like this. Look, isn't that a bit of overhanging rock showing through over there? Might there be stock under it?'

There was, and runaway wives and ringless fiancées were forgotten in the hard slog of beating the elements.

Thor and Juliana found themselves alone. Cosmo was busy with his survivors, proud of himself, Anthea was working with Jeff. Thor began to heave a sheep up, Juliana helping, her head close to his. 'Good girl,' he said. 'Commit yourself all you can. Get in really deep, then turn make-believe into reality. Because it *is* for real, and for ever.'

She said despairingly, in a low voice, 'Thor! You know why I'm doing it. You know why I'm going along with it at the moment. It's for Cosmo and Anthea's sake.'

They got the wether up, held it steadily, their faces almost touching over its back. He said intensely, 'Juliana, I told you about Johnny and Henrietta wasting some of the best years of their lives. Then it all came right, in these mountains, where both of them belonged . . . though their unhappiness had taken them all over the world, apart. Do you think I'm going to let history repeat itself and have *us* waste the best years of our lives?'

Her voice shook. 'Don't put such pressure on me. I *can't* marry you, Thor, and that's all there is to it. I *can't*!'

They were up to their knees in snow. Thor half straightened up, gripped one shoulder of hers and said, with eyes as bleak as the mountain tops, 'Are you—can you—be already married? Are you married to someone else?'

She looked directly at him. 'No, I'm not married—of course I'm not. That's not the only reason it could be.'

His face broke up and his smile was a conquering, all-powerful one. 'It's the only reason I'd accept. Don't fight the inevitable.'

She said helplessly, 'Thor, you're impossible!'

He laughed, then changed his tone, as if he'd actually settled something. 'Put Cosmo and Anthea into the Lake Tekapo room tonight. You've probably realised it's the only spare room with a double bed. I'm sure neither will mind that two walls have the original paper, one the new, and the other is half stripped! As soon as this snow is finished and done with, sweetheart, I'll finish papering it and I think we should have a new shower put in its bathroom. That one's rather old-fashioned now. They have some very posh cubicles now. All right by you?'

'It's nothing to do with me, and you know it.'

'It's everything to do with you, my love. It's going to be your bedroom, and mine, for the rest of our lives. Ah, you're blushing—that's hopeful! By the way, when you fly back this afternoon, don't forget Cosmo will expect you to kiss me goodbye. Make sure you make that kiss a convincing one!'

A tremor passed over Juliana, a wave of sweetness ... something that seemed to take possession of her. Could she withstand him? But she must.

They pushed more sheep along the track to their destination. Thor began whistling: 'Oh, who will o'er the downs so free, oh, who will with me ride? Oh, who will o'er the downs with me to win a bonnie bride?'

She caught his eye and wanted to laugh. He sang the words under his breath to her, 'Her father he has locked the door, her mother keeps the key, but neither doors nor locks shall keep my own true love from me.'

Juliana pretended she'd have to go all the way with her animal, which was in front. She didn't want Thor to notice the tears in her eyes ... there was no locked door, no hidden key ... no adamant father. There was a very dear father, who had been wrongly accused years ago when he was young and vulnerable and lonely. The father who must never know his daughter's steps had led her to the one place in the world he had wanted to forget . . . and had fallen in love with Thor of Thor's Hill!

Without thinking much of it, Juliana gave them all a moment of magic sandwiched in among the hard slog. The helicopter had landed on another hill across a cleft from them. They could see the three dark figures busy there. Thor wanted them all to come back to the hut for lunch at the one time. He cupped his hands about his mouth and yelled 'Coo-ee!' at them, but obviously his voice wasn't carrying that far, even in this clear stillness. Juliana said, 'I'll yodel for them if you like, Thor.'

He stared, so did the others, then he smiled. 'Of course . . . your Swiss grandparents. Go ahead.'

Jeff, Cosmo, Anthea and Thor were entranced as the silver and golden tones floated out across shining snow. She was so matter-of-fact about it, quite unaware of the picture it made. The men on the far mountainside swung round instantly, then as her yodelling ceased, danced up and down and waved their arms like semaphore flags to show they understood. It was only then that she turned to the others and realised she'd had a delighted audience. Cosmo said, 'What a pity we haven't got a television crew up here filming the rescue of Thor's Hill sheep for that programme . . . you know, *The High-country Men.* You would have made their day, Juliana. As it is, you've made mine, I know.'

'Mine too,' said Thor, and something in his voice turned Juliana's resolve to sever her life from this homestead to water. Those two words told her how much he loved her. She shied away from an answering wave of love for him within her, and said lightly, 'It just happened Grössvater taught us all from when we were very tiny, so we think nothing of it. He said if ever we were lost among his mountains or our Scots mountains, we could call for help. But to hear it in Switzerland, resounding from peak to peak, is really something.'

'Yours would do me,' said Jeff.

Back at the base, well pleased with their morning's work, they tramped back to the hut for their lunch. The big wide-mouthed flasks yielded thick soup they thinned down with boiling water; they ate huge slabs of mutton sandwiches, the scones Grizel had made early in the day, and, following Grizel's instructions, Juliana scraped a huge casserole of steak-and-kidney into an old iron pot, the replica of many she'd seen in cottages in Scotland, ready to be hooked on to the old-fashioned swee at one side of the fire that the men could swing back over the burning wood when the others had gone back to the homestead and the four of them would be left alone to continue their rescue work. The next day they would fry chops, leave potatoes in their jackets cooking in the ashes. Today was sheer luxury.

This time they left Cosmo and Anthea moving the sheep nearer at hand and Thor and Juliana took off on skis to discover more distant sheep-camps. The helicopter had done well with their drops of hay and nuts and Pete and Collard had marked the sites well. The sun was already thawing out the covering of snow on the northward faces, which boded well for the morrow when the four men would be able to work all day.

Juliana closed her mind to the fear of something happening to any one of them, isolated till the day after tomorrow. That was something mountain wives had to live with. What was she thinking? She wasn't going to be a mountain wife . . . by the time September was gone she'd be on her way back to Scotland and in no time this would be just a dear memory! But she knew so well the hazards of this sort of terrain. Severe frosts could harden the snow to a perilous crust, form a film of black ice over rocks that had been uncovered by that sun . . . she wished she could stay here, with the men.

It was wonderful to be on skis again, especially with such experts as these men whose skills had become part of their everyday winter lives. Their time was all too short now, the winter day wouldn't last much longer. The sun was westering now. Incredible to think that in a few moments, in that silvery bird waiting on the mountainside, they would have followed the dark course of the river to the homestead and all its creature comforts.

The moment came, as Thor had planned, when they

kissed goodbye. Juliana held out her hands very naturally, but he crushed her close, and she glimpsed over his shoulder the delighted looks on his men's faces as if they'd seen this coming . . . then, telling herself she was just obeying orders, she clung to him and returned kiss for kiss. As he lifted his mouth from hers he said exultantly, 'You beauty!' Then they were running for the helicopter. She turned just before she reached it, said over her shoulder: 'Take care.' She couldn't help herself.

Back at the homestead Don had done wonders with his snow-ploughing and Barbara and the children had more of the ewes into the huge covered yards, adjoining the woolshed which held many more. Don was still out with his dogs, droving the hoggets into the paddocks the ewes had vacated, and Barbara, Marian and the boys were feeding out from one of the smaller tractor and trailer outfits, to the cattle. Grizel had the fowls fed and shut up and George was keeping the big house warm for their return. The helicopter took off again very smartly and soared over Calamity Valley towards Craigievar.

Grizel and George were wonderful the way they played the genial hosts now. Grizel even looked with kind eyes upon Anthea. 'Juliana tells me you've worked like a Trojan this day, and that your man has too. All the more credit when it's work you're not accustomed to.'

Cosmo grinned, 'I admit I've a few sore muscles where I didn't even know I had muscles, but after the pressures of business, I've found it stimulating. When I was younger I used to have holidays on a farm in Northland, a dairy farm, and enjoyed it. It belonged to a mate of mine from boarding school. I believe he runs it now—I must look him up. How about it, Anthea? Having shown me what you can do, we'll try our hands at doing things we've never done together before.'

George, while the women did the dishes, took Cosmo off to the office, and found Cosmo's knowledge of business procedures and markets very helpful.

Then Juliana said, 'Thor said you two were to have his parents' sitting-room tonight. I'm having an early night, reading, after we get the second lot of news. I'll light that lamp in the sitting-room.'

At that identical moment all the lights in the house sprang on. They jumped, then clapped. 'I must admit I'm glad. Filling all those hotwater bottles is time-taking and they only give just a certain area of warmth. I'm all for electric blankets. I'll switch them all on now, in case it fails again. Grizel, will the men be able to see the homestead lit up?'

'They will. That hut is well up really. It doesn't look so high when you get there, but from here to there is a steep rise, with even the valley floor steadily ascending.'

'I wish they were here to share the comfort,' said Juliana wistfully.

Grizel shot a sly look at her face. 'Is that all you wish?' They all laughed, then Grizel said, 'Come half-past seven you'll probably know they've seen our lights. We'll signal each other from the snow-gear room at the end of the long porch. In the old days they used candles. Now we use torches, passing a piece of cardboard across the light in Morse code. Satisfy you?'

They all went. There was something fascinatingly primitive about it. Grizel sent a message: 'Is all well with you? All is well here.'

She slowly spelled their answer back to them, George writing it down. 'All well with us. Good show about the lights. See you day after tomorrow.' And it ended: 'Love.' Grizel looked Juliana straight in the eye. 'That's never been used as an ending before.' Cosmo guffawed happily.

Juliana lay awake a long time after she put her light out. She was restless, unsatisfied; something, an inner compulsion, was driving her. Finally she recognised it for what it was, an urge to write poetry. From her father she had inherited that imperative need at certain times in her life. She lay back thinking of Thor ... of his audacious words about the Lake Tekapo room, and her mind toyed with the dream of fulfilment that meant ... its delicate turquoise shades, its view of the Two Thumb Range in the distance, the soft hangings, the wide, low bed ... Thor's voice: 'Because it's real, *and for ever.*' That would be true, if that other barrier didn't stand between them, it would be for ever, as lasting as his mountains.

She thought of his goodbye kiss, of the dark speck of his figure against the whiteness of the snow as their helicopter rose into the sky ... of the dangers up there ... if only she could have stayed with him!

Her writing pad was on the bedside table. She reached across, picked it up, seized a ballpoint and found herself writing:

> '*My heart is on the hill with you, man of the mountain ways,*
> *Where wild and treacherous the storms, and filled with fear my days;*
> *God keep you safe, my love, my own, from harm and danger free,*
> *Till, when the dragging hours are done, homeward you come to me.*'

She looked at it a long time, comforted by having put it into words, then, suddenly angry with herself for dreaming, tore the page out of the pad, fired it into the wastepaper basket, and snapped off her light.

They *were* dragging hours, even though they were filled with a multitude of tasks without and within. One moment Juliana was thankful they had the two guests to take her mind off his absence, then she dreaded Thor's return, with him determined to take up where they had laid their relationship down. She just couldn't tell the folk here that if she married Thor, her father would never visit her home, that she might never see him again. She herself might know, beyond a shadow of doubting, that her father wasn't a thief, never had been, but *he* would never be sure that anyone else believed him. And it would get out that the Todd Powers who'd tried to get away with the Thor's Hill gold all those years ago was none less than Fergus Hendrie. It would have been common knowledge round Tekapo and Mount Cook.

There was no way out. No way she dared risk linking her life with Thor's Hill. Dad had been courageous enough, all those years ago, to carve out a new life for himself, to revert to his own name, and to make it count for something. It wasn't for his daughter to bring him low now. As soon as she could reasonably do so, she would go from here. A thought struck her. When dear old George had given her that tiny phial of raw gold for her birthday, and she'd asked him was it Thor's Hill gold, he'd said he wasn't sure, but he hoped it would bring her more happiness than the man who'd won that gold from the mountains. What did that mean? Oh, probably nothing. She supposed some rough old character up here had found it and sold it to George, and perhaps he'd thought the money hadn't done him much good in the end. She felt uneasily that she was beginning to be a bit obsessed by the thought of raw gold. She tore her mind away from that, made herself plan how she would get away from here when river and snow no longer kept her from the outside world.

It seemed to her she moved in a time-bubble, as if everything was compressed within the circle of the next few weeks. She must endure them till at last she was free to go.

The day of the helicopter's return came. It landed, took on board more feed, and the pilot said, looking at the sun in the northern sky, blindingly brilliant and quite hot, 'I'd like them off the hill now, it's just the weather for avalanches.'

Juliana said, 'I didn't want to say that to the Ramsays, though they'll know it well enough, but I've found myself listening every time I've gone outside.'

Cosmo said admiringly, 'We'd never have known you were anxious. You've sure got what it takes for up here!' She smiled and moved away from him. She didn't want Cosmo starting to ask questions about how long it would be before she and Thor got married, or too many questions about her mother and father. Cosmo said to the pilot, 'We'll be all ready when you get back from this lift. Believe me, we're most grateful to you. I can't

e away from business too long, and my wife hadn't
argained on being cooped up here when she dropped
1 on them—she'd forgotten how dicey it can be. But
'm glad we had this experience with you chaps. I'm
fraid that from now on, whenever we see conditions
ke this on television, I'll bore all my friends to death,
elling them how we were marooned here and helped
escue the merinos. Incidentally, if ever you fellows are
p in Auckland, give us a ring and come out to see us.
here's only one Rosenby in the phone book.'

At last it was over, the men were back, Operation
Iaylift was completed. The guests began to depart,
aying their farewells and thanks. Thor was loading
nutton into the machine as a parting gift for the men.
As he came back to Juliana, Anthea dashed back to the
wo of them, looking mischievous, then said to Thor,
Don't forget to make Julie tell you why I made a point
f telling her I lied about Robert Herrick. Her reaction
o that would have flattered you.' Then she went
unning off to join Cosmo, who was looking back for
er. Thor looked puzzled, said to Juliana, 'What's all
nat about?'

She shrugged, 'Nothing really ... oh, look, they're
ff!'

uliana felt she walked a tightrope. Thor, to her, was
npredictable. How was he going to continue? Would
be from where they'd left off, on that snowy
nountainside? Perhaps he thought they needed a break
n hostilities. Oh, how stupid, they weren't hostile. But
needed a breathing-space, a lessening of tension.

The roar of the avalanches was heard now,
pectacular if one could distinguish the spray and
moke of the particles of snow rising afterwards, but
ery awesome even if one was accustomed to it. Sooner
r later the snow-melt would find its way into the
Rubicon. Every morning Juliana slipped up to the
ookout to scan the river. It rose and fell according to
he thaw, or a succeeding hard frost. She didn't analyse
er feelings, but knew an unworthy sense of relief as it
ontinued to be uncrossable.

She'd sent letters out, by the helicopter, to he
parents, and knew they would just bear the Moun
Cook postmark. She'd chatted on in them quit
impersonally, sounding just like any tourist, and heade
her letter Mount Cook Post Office. She had describe
Lake Tekapo, the Mackenzie Country, the Tasma
glacier, doing it all from a brochure she'd found in th
office; said how she was enjoying the skiing in th
powdery snow. She might go on to Queenstown nex
she said, as she felt she must see all these glacial lakes i
their gorgeous colours. From that they'd never suspec
her real whereabouts.

Thor was friendly, even fun, but there were no mor
tender moments. Yet with it all Juliana never felt as
he'd given up. With George needing less and les
attention she spent a lot of time across at the Murray
helping Barbie, especially with Jemmie. Sometimes sh
slipped across in the evenings, and Don brought he
home. She said Barbie was appreciating the feminin
company.

The river began to subside a little, the roar of th
avalanches became less frequent. She and Barbara wer
sitting darning one night when Thor walked in. 'I'v
been across at the cookhouse. Willocks needed som
papers signed that came in with that bag of mail th
chopper brought. He wants them ready for when th
river's fordable. Pete had the bright idea that as soon a
it is I'd let him cross on his horse and go down countr
for the mail. These distant girl-friends! I said I'd hav
the hide off the first man who attempted it before th
grader comes up. I was in touch with the grader-drive
today by phone. Usually at this time of year, we'r
coming and going as we please, but today I saw th
ground cracking for the daffodil spears and buds on th
willows. I'm grateful for the deciduous trees. If it wa
nothing but Corsican and Douglas firs and pines, an
the New Zealand bush back in the gullies, we'd hardl
know spring was round the corner.' He looked across a
Juliana. 'When you hear the shining cuckoo, you'
know it's here.'

'Do they come in great numbers?' she asked.

'No, they only pause on their way to more
temperate zones, but soon the dotterels and the
oyster-catchers will be round the streams in the
river-bed, and stilts. But when the grader's been up to
firm up the ford, our social life will begin again ...
surprising how much coming and going there is once
we have access. And of course we must get you to
Mount Cook. You heard how keen the helicopter
boys were to get Fergus Hendrie's daughter there. I
wouldn't be surprised if they put on a dance for
you—at Tekapo too, probably. We'll all go up to the
Hermitage for that. Willocks won't bother, so he can
look after the place. I daresay it'll come off early
October.'

Juliana snipped off her wool and pulled the heel of
Don's enormously thick farm socks into shape, thinking
to herself she could be on her way back to Scotland
then. She'd skip seeing any more of New Zealand. If
Thor knew she was back in the Northern Hemisphere,
he'd have to give up, but if she stayed in New Zealand
he would pursue her.

She had twisted her smooth golden hair into a French
pleat and anchored it with a clasp her grandmother had
given her, a very old-fashioned enamel one, of a row of
gentians, deeply blue, with tufts of white edelweiss in
between. She was wearing a blue woollen dress in a soft,
fine material, that made her eyes look almost blue. It
had a soft cowl neckline, that was looped below the
shoulders with tiny gold chains and pearl studs. Her
Swiss belt with its multi-coloured studs on a black
background was clipped about her waist and laced
together with more gold chains that fell almost to its
hem. Thor's eyes surveyed her long, beautiful legs and
the high-heeled black shoes she was wearing. 'You're
going to have a wonderful time going back home along
the track in those.'

She made a face at him. 'Stupid ... I've got my fur-
lined boots with me for walking back, and my parka. If
I'd only had these I'd never have got here. I just felt like
being more feminine tonight. Barbie and I decided
today that we'd had enough of utility garments, thick

trews, and chunky sweaters and things, so that's why
we're all dressed up.'

Don surveyed his wife, 'And very nice too. I
approve.'

'So too do I,' said Thor, sunk deeply in his chair,
looking as if he was very content to relax. It was a
merry hour, finishing up with a sing-song round the
piano, with Marian rushing out from her bedroom to
join in. Some were songs Juliana didn't know, songs of
the shearing-sheds and the blacksmiths' shops of this
back-country, born in the days when entertainment up
here was nil, and had to be manufactured by
themselves. Juliana, as they ended, said, 'How this
reminds me of sitting round camp-fires in the
mountains, and folk-songs being sung. I was so lucky
going on two or three expeditions with Mother and
Dad.' She felt tears sting the back of her eyes and
wouldn't let them fall. She looked away quickly. Thor,
getting up from the piano, touched her hand briefly.
She was grateful. There were times when a touch could
mean everything.

CHAPTER TEN

THERE was everything of sheer beauty in the Alpine night when they stepped outside, clear, cold, sparkling, with a moon that looked like a backdrop to a stage, so perfectly round, so glowingly golden. A night to quicken heartbeats, to set the pulses throbbing with that indefinable alchemy for two people in love. Juliana hoped Thor would do nothing to make her yield to its magic insistency. In cold daylight she knew she couldn't marry him; on such a night as this, she was afraid she might consent.

But they walked in silence, just his hand under her elbow to help her over the rough patches. But it was a potent silence. It was only as Thor opened the door that he spoke. 'We'll go into my sitting-room, Juliana. We don't use it half enough. No doubt Grizel and George are tactfully in bed, but the living-room's got so many doors into it one always fears interruption.'

She knew a moment of apprehension. She'd been so grateful for this lull in pressure. If Thor became impatient she might have to leave here soon. She said, 'I'm not sure that that's a good idea, Thor, to settle down again. It's late.'

He smiled, the corners of the mouth she'd once thought stern lifting. 'I know. I want it to be late, we're always cluttered up with other people otherwise. There's something I want to ask you.'

She said unhappily, 'I wish you wouldn't.'

His eyes were smiling too. 'I know what you think. It's not that, just something I'm curious about. Come on, I'm determined. I'll carry you in if you don't come willingly.'

Juliana shrugged, 'All right. But I may not know the answer.'

'You know the answer all right.'

He must have set the scene before he went across to

the cookhouse. The fire had been lit earlier and wa
now glowing red to its heart. A deep chair was draw
up and a stool beside it.

Juliana looked at the proximity doubtfully, whic
made him laugh. 'It's all right, I'll play fair and ask yo
the question before I get you settled there. I know it'
sheer curiosity, but what did Anthea mean when sh
said she must tell you she lied about Robert Herrick
Who the dickens is Robert Herrick?'

Juliana stared, then made her gamin face at him, the
laughed, 'Oh, Thor, you're so unexpected! I thought i
was something important. Robert Herrick is—was—
poet. I rather think he was born in the sixteent
century. He was a clergyman, and wrote some quit
choice love-poems. One was to an Anthea. But wha
Anthea said was nothing, Thor, it was just a silly littl
attempt to sow a few seeds of doubt and jealousy, whe
she found you'd got over her a long time since, that'
all. It didn't matter to me, of course. I've met that typ
before, the kind who like to take the gilt off th
gingerbread when they see someone else being happy.'

The tawny eyes lit up. 'Then she did recognise you
happiness?'

Too late Juliana realised that had certainly been a
admission. She said hastily, 'Now, Thor, you made i
plain to her, didn't you, that you were interested in m
and it was too late for her to make a comeback?'

'I did. But not just to spike Anthea's guns. It wasn'
makebelieve with me, just a little premature. Neverthe
less, Anthea knew you—that you were not indifferent
Don't divert me. What *did* she mean. What *was* the lie?

The thick fair lashes swiftly veiled her eyes from him
As she studied her toes she said, 'Oh, several times sh
looked back, nostalgically, to the days when you adore
her.'

'When I thought I adored her,' he corrected.

'All right, when you thought it. Thor, I understood
You weren't much more than a boy, and lonely.
understand it because now I think I must have bee
madly lacking in discrimination to fall for Marcus. I
didn't last. It was built on a very slight attraction.'

'What was the lie?'

She laughed a laugh of pure merriment. 'George was writing to one of his daughters one night. You know how he adds a page regularly, then a whole budget goes off with the mail when it can be got out? He was after a quotation he couldn't quite recall. Like my dad, I take a small volume of Palgrave's Golden Treasury wherever I go, so I brought it out and left it there. Anthea picked it up when I was getting him to bed, and later on, she pretended to wipe away a tear. I asked her what was the matter and she sniffed and said, "So foolish of me . . . just that when Tulloch and I were in that first flush of falling for each other he said that Robert Herrick could have written that poem to me, not to his long-ago Anthea." That's all it was, Thor.'

'*All?* I came to know long ago that Anthea was a nasty piece of work, but I didn't think she'd stoop that low.'

Juliana shook her head at him. 'Now, Thor, she's had a complete change of heart. Do her the credit of taking it back. She needn't have.'

'Ye-es, but she could have thrown an almighty spanner into the works. Juliana, tell me, I've got to know so I can refute it if mischief was made . . . did she spill out other horrible doubts into your ear, not just a stupid one about poetry, but anything at all that may have caused you to hold back from entirely committing yourself?'

Again he saw the shadow pass over her face. 'No, I can't give you any reason for that, Thor, but it's a strong one. It lies right back in the past.'

His reaction was swift. 'Juliana, if there's something you're afraid to tell me, please try me. I'll try to understand.'

She looked puzzled, then her face cleared. 'Oh, no, Thor, nothing like that. No deep relationships in my past that could complicate things.'

'Then nothing else can matter. No former marriage, no affair. All right, I can wait. I've been swept off my feet and expect you to be too.' He caught her hands, looked whimsical and said, 'What a wooing! Juliana,

I'm a fool. Most chaps make a different approach—
they can take a girl out, go to plays, operas, concerts
Take her picnicking, moonlight rambling, visit her
friends, meet her people.'

At that last phrase he felt her flinch very slightly. He
continued, 'See her in her own home ... here we've had
to live under the same roof, endure hardship, isolation
suffer the pinpricks of the unwelcome Anthea ... it
hasn't been the norm at all. And look the way we
started off! I was flaming mad that some stiff and
starchy nurse from London could decide George was
well enough to be taken up to the back of beyond. I'd
no idea *how* you knew alpine conditions, or how good a
nurse you were. Lord, I even had the nerve to order you
not make mischief among my men! All right, my love
I'll give you time. I'll start behaving rationally, though I
don't feel rational ... I want you for my wife ... and
soon. But I'll behave. From now on I'll start to court
you—a trial period.

'Your parents are in a place about as remote as this. I
expect you to sever your world in half, to take on my
world without my seeing yours. Travel is nothing to
your people. If they can possibly free themselves from
the sort of engagements that must crowd in on them, is
there any reason they shouldn't fly here before going
home? It's easy—Bombay, Singapore, Auckland,
Christchurch, Mount Cook. If that flaming river rises,
I'll fly them in by helicopter. It would be nothing to
them. Or if you feel you must visit your home first, I'll
let you go, but——' his eyes narrowed, 'I'd follow you.
At least in your own surroundings you wouldn't feel
bulldozed into a quick decision. How about that,
sweetheart?'

Gratefully she said, summoning a smile, 'I think it
would be wise.' That would be the way to play it. Get
away from here, then, by letter, make it plain she had
no intention of returning. Then Dad's secret would be
safe, always.

He seemed to accept that. The whole strong face
softened, and, drawing her to the hearthrug, he said,
'Then let's start our courting. Because we're hemmed in

by mountains and rivers, I can't take you out and bring
you home, but at least tonight we were visiting, and
came home under a peerless moon, so let's pretend this
is your home and we're having a lingering goodnight;
I'll take the chair, you lean against my knee. We won't
talk about anything controversial, just happy, everyday
things.'

Bemused, Juliana allowed him to do just that. Thor
settled her on the stool, she leaned back, put an arm
across his knees, looked up and wrinkling her nose at
him asked, 'Such as what?'

He looked mock-reproachful. 'You're trying to put
me off my stride! That's supposed to kill conversation
stone dead ... looking for a topic. But you won't stop
me. We'll always have things to say to each other,
liebling.'

She caught her breath in at that. 'Oh, Thor, using
that word of endearment, you've whisked me back to
Lake Lucerne, and my grandparents' home. How come
you know the German word for darling?'

He leaned forward towards her upturned eager face.
'When the snows unlock their grip and the river
behaves itself, I'll take you over to Dragonshill, because
Charles and Francis Beaudonais-Smith own it. They
were the grandsons of old Madame Beaudonais, whose
only daughter married a Carl Schmidt, a German.
Francis and Charles both call their wives, Penny and
Hilary, by German and French endearments. We see a
lot of them normally. I knew your grandparents live in
the German-speaking part of Switzerland. Johnny and
Henrietta are pretty fluent in it too. It may keep you
from being too homesick.'

He was pretty sure of himself, this man of thunder.
She put a finger against his lips. 'No controversial
subjects, you said, Thor.'

She hadn't known that craggy face could look so
tender. 'Then I'll just say the things I've been wanting
to say this long time since.'

His finger traced the line of her nose. 'I told you once
I liked that little sprinkling of freckles. I also like how
fair and thick and straight your lashes are. I'd like to

see them on your cheeks some day as you lie asleep. But none of what makes me love you belongs to feature by feature ... it's the lights changing in your eyes, that very mobile mouth of yours. I never know whether it's going to crinkle into laughter or tighten into reproof ... like when I first met you. You sure were sparking on all cylinders, and then I had this ridiculous thought.' He paused, his eyes smiling.

Juliana couldn't help it. 'What thought?'

'That what fun it would be to fight with you. I looked on my mother and father as rather an ideal couple, yet I've seen Mother in right royal rages—and the next moment crumpling into irresistible giggles because she knew perfectly well she was being absurd and unreasonable. Like the mountains she lived among, she was either incredibly serene or wild and tempestuous.'

He slipped off the chair on to the rug. 'You're far too far away if I stay up there, decorously. No, don't pull away. This is courting, or it ought to be. All tendernesses and caresses ... what *are* you laughing at?'

She turned her head into his shoulder. 'I can't help it. You've just called me wild and tempestuous, and tender caresses sounded such a contrast.'

He laughed with her. 'That's what this sort of relationship is all about. Oh, my darling, *how* I love you when you're like this!'

His kiss was hard and demanding and under the strength and fire of the response he evoked, she was incapable of thinking how foolish this was, that it had no future, that it wasn't fair to him, that she mustn't encourage moments like this.

His laugh, when at last he let her come up for air, was exultant, tender. 'This is the right technique for sure,' he vowed recklessly, then she hid her face against him, this time to stem the endearments she wanted to utter. Once she let one spill out there would be no stopping her.

She felt his fingers pulling out the pins in her hair so that it fell all about her. 'I haven't seen you with your hair down since that time in the office when Rebecca was speaking to me.'

His hands came under her hair, each side of her neck, fluffed up her hair, pale and shining. The huge log that had been so slow-burning crashed in a shower of sparks. They looked at it, then at each other, and a tide of longing, unexpected and almost frightening in its intensity swept Juliana. It made her tremble physically. She said uncertainly, 'Thor . . . I think we must . . .' Her voice trailed off.

He nodded. 'Yes, we must, I know. Time to stop. It's not easy, this living under the same roof, without the intimacies of marriage. But I'm sure this hour has shown you that ours *must* be a continuing and deepening relationship. It can't be otherwise.'

He drew her to her feet, and they stood looking at each other. As Juliana went to speak Thor shook his head at her. 'Don't spoil it, my love, with saying the same reason still exists against it, that it can't be a continuing one. Don't lie awake mulling over it. If you must tease your mind with something, try planning a future together.' His laugh was pure mischief. 'Like deciding which church it shall be in. The Church of the Good Shepherd, on its headland jutting into Lake Tekapo, your parish church in Scotland, or some church on the shores of Lake Lucerne? It can be wherever you want it, but if it's here, I'll see to it that your whole family comes!'

She said swiftly, 'Goodnight, Thor. Not a controversial hour, you promised me, so just goodnight.'

As she put her hand on the door-knob she thought of something, came back and said, 'And thank you, Thor, for understanding how I felt tonight when I said the sing-song recalled our sing-songs round our camp-fires. I appreciated that. But then I thought how foolish it was of me to feel even a vestige of sadness, when you can't still share those things with your parents.'

He did not touch her then. He just said, 'Thank you. That's my girl,' and let her go.

Her last conscious thought was that she dared not let herself think about churches . . . weddings . . . and that fine though his offer had been to bring her whole family here, that was a promise that could never be fulfilled, because her father would never, never return to Thor's Hill.

Juliana was grateful that he slackened the pace a little the next few days. He seemed to spend what time he could, inside, in the office. A tremendous amount of farm business, of course, was done on the telephone, because of distances and accessibility involved. The days, anyway, were still incredibly busy and tough outside, feeding vast amounts out to the hungry stock, though every day the skies grew clearer, the sun stronger, the snow thinner . . . and the Rubicon fell a little more. When she found herself hoping there'd be more avalanches to swell it again, she took herself to task.

The women on the other sheep-stations rang her frequently and even the ones she hadn't met seemed like old, dear friends. Charles and Francis Beaudonais-Smith each had a conversation with her in German, just for the fun of it. She loved these gestures, yet each one stabbed her, knowing that she couldn't remain to be part of this scene.

Then came the night when in the big kitchen-living-room they were all reading. They'd fancied nothing on the radio and reading was an integral part of the life up here. She was enjoying the bookshelves in Thor's sitting-room, the old books and the new. She was deep in a story of the Mediterranean when the phone rang. Despite the snow and heights outside, she was on the Côte d'Azur, winding along above the blue sea, with the pastel-washed villas a-foam with scarlet and pink geraniums bordering the road and a hot sun beating down on the terraces.

She scarcely lifted her head as Thor answered the phone, then something in his voice and in the passage of time before he was connected made her look at him sharply. It must be a toll call, long-distance. But she mustn't appear curious, though certainly Grizel and George weren't bothering to hide their interest . . . they had both laid their books down.

There was something in Thor's voice, something vital, excited. He said, 'Yes, Thor's Hill here, South Canterbury. Yes, I'll hang on.' Then, 'Oh, hullo, sir. I hoped this might be you. Glad you could make the call so soon—it could have taken days for my message to reach you. Yes, my name is Tulloch MacNair. Yes, she's fine, in fact, you could say blooming. What did you say? Oh, what's she doing up here? Nursing my cousin through a fairly long convalescence. She was nursing in the hospital he was in, in Timaru, and when he knew she was planning a Mount Cook trip, persuaded her to accompany him. My cousin's name? George Ramsay. His sister Grizel is his housekeeper and I'm a distant cousin. We're joint owners. I thought it was time your Juliana was in touch with you.' Out of the corner of his eye he saw Juliana get to her feet, staring.

He listened to the voice at the other end, then said, 'Yes, I thought you'd find it a great coincidence ... Juliana's told me your home in the Highlands is called Ben Thor. I think that too attracted her to this place. Because of the similarity that's why I worded the message to ring Tulloch Macnair of Thor's Hill, South Canterbury, New Zealand, in case you thought it an urgent call from your family at Ben Thor ...'

Juliana was aghast. What a terrible thing, for Dad to have a shock like this! To know that a daughter, who'd written as from Mount Cook Village, was actually living at the very place where, when he was a lad of eighteen, his record had been blotted. She felt petrified.

Thor said, 'Before I hand the phone over to her, sir, there's something I'd like to tell you. She hasn't accepted me as yet, but I'm hoping to marry your daughter. Naturally she wants time. I feel she's so cut off from her family, from her old life, that I want to ask you if you and her mother could visit New Zealand before you return to Scotland. I think you'd find this area very interesting to you. Ed Hillary climbed round here before he tackled Everest, you know. Is there any chance you can make it?'

He listened again, laughed. 'Yes, I realise it must be a

bit of a shock, coming like this, but we're so cut off at
the moment. We got a bit of mail in and some sent out
when we had a helicopter in to do a hay-lift to our
stock, but before that we were incommunicado. Is Mrs
Hendrie going to speak to Juliana too? Oh, what a pity.
But get her to ring when she joins you and of course
make it collect ... or do you say reverse the charges?
It's easier than at your end, I suppose. Here she is, sir,
your darling daughter, just about ready, by now, to tear
the phone off me!'

Fergus Hendrie's darling daughter took hold of the
phone as if it had been a rattlesnake, and in a wobbly,
scared voice said: 'Dad?'

She felt his voice, in answer, was also strange.
'Juliana, what *is* all this about? Oh, darling, it's
wonderful to hear you—but how, oh, how did you get
to Thor's Hill of all places?'

She was intensely aware of the audience of three.
What could she say that wouldn't give too much away?
In the pause her father said, 'Was it simply coincidence,
Juliana? I must know!'

She said then quite simply, 'No, it wasn't, Dad. It
was of intent.' She heard his indrawn breath as plainly
as if he'd been standing beside her, and made her voice
sound matter-of-fact. 'Dad, hang on a moment. I'll go
to the office phone.'

She put her hand over the mouthpiece and said
appealingly, 'You won't think me rude, will you? I'd—
I'd——'

Thor said swiftly, 'Of course, I should have sent you
through there.'

George rose to his feet and said, 'I'd like fine to
speak to Fergus Hendrie ... may I?'

Juliana was on her way but heard Thor say, 'Of
course ... don't hurry it, George, it's being charged to
us. I left the message thataway.'

She sped to the office, carefully shut the door, seated
herself at Thor's desk, picked up the phone to hear
George saying: 'Man, I'm tickled pink to be speaking to
Fergus Hendrie. We've not known very long who you
were. Your daughter had some bee in her bonnet about

wanting people to like her for herself alone, not because she had a famous father. But Thor ... Tulloch ... tumbled to it. We've got your books, every one of them. Now, sir, I heard what Tulloch said to you. Your lassie has won all hearts up here, but my young cousin is finding the going hard for some reason, though it's as plain as a pikestaff they're made for each other. I'd like to endorse Thor's invitation. Come over, and make it soon. It's a father's privilege, and a mother's, to look us over. Now I'd better let you speak to your lassie.'

Juliana said, 'Dad, just a moment. Er ... the kitchen receiver's down. Dad, before we discuss what we must discuss, how are you, and how's Mother?' She was told, then her father said, 'Now, dear girl, with no one listening in, can you tell me what you meant about going to Thor's Hill with intent?'

'Will you hear me out, Dad? Don't interrupt till I get it all out. I'd always wondered why you talked so little about your early life in New Zealand. I knew you were somewhere inland from Timaru, that's all, so I took a position in Timaru. I loved old George Ramsay when I nursed him. Then one day when some of the nurses and patients were talking about the topsy-turvy seasons here, I was just about turned to stone when George quoted your July poem, and said it had been written by a little adopted boy on the station, who'd had lessons with his daughters. I couldn't believe it.

'I thought I'd go on up to Mount Cook, spend some time there, ring up the station and see if it was possible to visit it so I could find out more, but when George found I was taking my holidays there, he begged me to go with him while he convalesced. I felt it was Providential, Dad, that I was being led. Dad, they still have your poem, framed, on the wall, in the kitchen. They still speak of you with affection. The married couple on the farm, though they'd never met you, of course, named their little son Todd, after Todd Powers who had written that poem.

'But—but it was only recently, when a visitor arrived here by helicopter and got stuck here because of weather, that I found out why you left here as a young man, and had never returned. No, Dad, don't speak yet, because I want you to know that I know beyond shadow of doubting, that you were wrongly accused! I haven't dared question anyone or seem too interested. You're a world figure and nothing must ever smirch your name. If you said you won that gold from the ground on your holidays, then you did. I've got a positive feeling that if Polly and George had been here, it wouldn't have gone the way it did. That it would've been thrashed out, they'd have got to the bottom of it. They'd have believed you. You've been mentioned several times and George said once that Polly yearned after you the rest of her life ... yes, Dad, she died a few years ago. All right, Dad, I'll stop now.'

Fergus's voice was rough with emotion, yet tender for this loved daughter who believed in him. 'Juliana, I had heard from a man who'd once spent months up there, wintering wild cattle, that away beyond Skippers Canyon, you could still find gold, not in large quantities, but payable. Like any young lad trying to make his way, I dreamed of a lucky strike. I didn't get it, just dust and a few small nuggets, but enough to be happy about. I didn't tell a soul because the beauty and remoteness of that area at the back of beyond got to me. I didn't want even another minor gold rush started that would despoil the area and break men's hearts because there wasn't enough of it.

'But I wanted it assayed, and had the idea, too, that if other samples of metals I'd obtained proved interesting, I might be retained by one of the international companies to go prospecting for these other minerals. Just a dream. I longed, in those days, to go exploring, to break fresh ground.

'Juliana, *that* bag of gold in my kit wasn't mine. It had been substituted for mine. You can't identify dust, of course, but there were small nuggets in it, quite individual shapes. One bit was quite squiggly, easily recognisable. It simply wasn't there. I was going to have that bit made into a pendant for Polly. But this gold was the bag George Ramsay had always kept in his safe for sheer sentiment's sake. His father had washed it out over the years. He had shown it to plenty of people, me included. Someone had obviously got away with mine, and wanted me blamed for the other, so I'd be turned off in the Ramsays' absence. So thank you for believing in your father without an explanation. Juliana, what did you say?'

'I said that George and Polly tried to have you traced—tried for years. When I knew that, although George was just mentioning you as a young shepherd they'd been fond of, not as a delinquent, I knew you must have changed your name back to your rightful one, and that the Todd the Powers couple called you was short for Talbot. But it's all right, Dad, as soon as the river goes down and we can get George safely over, with Grizel, and down to Fairlie, I'll fly home. I found out what I came to find, and I'm only sorry it's revived for you some bitter memories.'

'Juliana, you must do nothing in a hurry,' said her father. 'You must have overheard Tulloch MacNair saying he wanted to marry you but you hadn't accepted him yet. I appreciated him getting in touch with me. I want to know this: Do you love him? Do you want to marry him?'

Juliana caught her breath in. The voice at the other end said, 'I've got my answer: silence gives assent. Why haven't you accepted him? Is it because if I come to see where my daughter is to live, I'll be recognised? Is that it? Is that all? Or is there some other reason?'

'Isn't it enough, Dad? I could never do that to you— never. You made a new start, created a fine life for yourself, made a wonderful family atmosphere for us three children, took us on minor safaris when you'd have gone further and faster alone. I've got to get out of here, Dad, get back home. It won't always be as—as bad as it seems at this moment.'

'My darling daughter! There's no need for such finality in your tone. I'd like to consult with Astrid. Your mother knows, of course; I told her before I married her. It happened a long time ago, you know. At the time I felt my life was blighted, but now I wonder if it hadn't been for that cruel injustice of long ago, and I admit it *was* cruel, would I ever have pitted myself against the mountains of the world in an endeavour to forget those mountains I loved most of all; would I ever have met your mother? Darling, I'm sorry Astrid won't be with me for a couple of days yet. Meantime, do nothing rash. As a family we know how to wait, about sitting it out ... in tents in alpine snows, waiting for a storm to abate, waiting for news from some hazardous expedition ... it's not always been easy on my family, but at least you've all got what it takes. Perhaps now I may be able to repay a little of what my family has had to endure for my sake. I'm going to say goodbye now, lass, because I feel badly at staying on the line so long at someone else's expense. I'll say goodnight and God bless, my dear. I'll give you your mother's customary greeting because she's not here to give it to you ... May God hold you in the hollow of His hand.'

The next moment Juliana was staring at the instrument in her hand, her father's voice cut off. She replaced the receiver.

Footsteps approached, Thor's. He flung open the door, his eyes alight. 'Well ... well, Juliana? Did I do right?'

She knew she couldn't quench that light in his eyes. He'd planned this to give her pleasure, to bring her two worlds together. She said brokenly, 'It was wonderful, Thor. Th-thank you.'

He put his arms about her and said smilingly, 'I think those tears are for joy. I also knew it was time your family heard from me.' Then his smile faded and he said urgently, 'Does it make any difference?'

'To why I won't marry you?'

He said levelly, 'Why you *think* you won't marry me.'

Juliana swung away from him and gazed out of the window. 'Thor ... we agreed to wait. To mark time.'

His arms came about her from the back, clasping his hands together at her breast. 'I did agree that, sweetheart.'

She twisted round in his embrace, 'Bear with me, Thor. Thank you for getting in touch with my father. He's going to ring again when Mother joins him.' She took one of the strong hands, rubbed it against her cheek, then walked out of the office.

Her very feelings and thoughts seemed suspended from then on. She dared not let herself hope, yet that matchless comfort of hearing her father's voice had sown a tiny seed. But that was a relic from childhood days, she told herself . . . days when Dad was Mr Fix-it. When he could make all things come right, from broken dolls to skinned knees.

She spent most of the day in the schoolroom over at Barbie's. She wanted tasks that would take her away from Thor. Barbie noticed her restlessness and said, 'Juliana, what is it? I think you're like my Don when he's got something on his mind. He prowls. You didn't have to offer to clean out the storeroom, you know, when lessons were finished. But you can't sit still. Is it love taking you that way?'

It was a relief to admit it. Barbie said, 'And the course isn't running smoothly?'

'It's not even just rough, Barbie . . . it's an obstacle race, and one obstacle is unsurmountable!'

'Obstacles are always overcome eventually. I won't probe. But I'll put my money on Thor. He'll never give up. Pet, would it be easier if you stayed here for dinner? Or would that be the wrong thing to do?'

'It would be right. I'm so tempted to rush my fences, and I mustn't. I'm filling in time for my parents to ring from India. That won't be till tomorrow.' She had to explain her tension somehow.

Barbara took pity on her and stopped questioning. She handed her an overall. 'Put this back on and help me peel the potatoes. Don said he hoped you stay on and have a game of Scrabble with us later.'

Scrabble! When she felt her whole fate hung in the balance!

At nine the phone rang; Don answered it. 'Sure, boss, I'll bring her over right away.' He turned. 'Thor wants you. He says you're to go to his sitting-room—there's a message from your parents. I wonder why he didn't switch them through here, it's easy enough. Perhaps he was too scared, seeing it was from such a distance, in case he'd cut them off. It could be you're to ring them back. I daresay the timing is tricky.'

Juliana had on the blue dress again, with the embroidered belt and the swinging gilt cords. She pulled her hooded jacket over it and Don started up. 'Just drop me at the bottom of the terrace steps.'

He shook his head. 'No fear! If it happens you've got to ring them back, you won't want to be out of breath. I'll go right up.'

She went swiftly through the front doors and along the concrete porch to the kitchen. George and Grizel were by the fireplace, looking as bland as their expressive faces would let them. To give her courage to face whatever the message was, she looked instinctively to where the poem hung on the wall. It was gone! What could that mean?

'Straight through,' said George. 'He's waiting for you.'

The sitting-room looked exactly as it had done that other night.

Thor was on the hearthrug. She couldn't read the look on his face. He was holding something in his hands. It caught, then riveted her attention. It—it was, of all things, the framed poem!

He said nonchalantly, 'I think it's up to you to decide where this should hang. This will be the room we'll spend most of our time in. Your father's poem should have pride of place. You know, I didn't hear it wrong that morning. You *did* say: "Good morning, *Dad*." '

Juliana couldn't speak. She closed her eyes against the impact of it. She opened them again and he was just the same, still holding that poem. She found her voice. 'You know . . . you know that my father was little Todd Powers. That he——'

Thor said, his voice clear and slow, enunciating every word so she could take it in, 'We know, we *all* know, that Fergus Hendrie is the young shepherd who suffered a grave injustice when he was only eighteen years old, at the hands of the men who were here then. Oh, darling, darling, if we'd only known!'

She was bewildered, uncomprehending. 'What do you mean? Oh, how can you know? Oh, Thor, how?'

He put the frame down carefully, on a little table, came to her, took her hands and said, 'Your father just rang ... he told me exactly why you thought you couldn't marry me. He said he and your mother will be here in a few days and if he was convinced you really loved me, he wouldn't let the shadow of what happened years ago stand in our way, that no matter who believed him guilty, it mustn't stand in the way of his daughter's happiness. Oh, my love, I'm telling it so badly! He started off by saying he could tell me why you wouldn't accept me, that it was because he was Todd Powers, who reverted to his own name shortly after he left here. It just about took the legs from under me. But before I could say what this knowledge would mean to George, who'd tried every possible avenue to trace the young Todd, I realised *he* didn't know ... that *you* didn't know his name had been cleared long ago.'

Juliana's eyes were like stars, her lips parted. She breathed: 'But how—how?'

Thor's hands holding hers, were pounding life and vitality and hope into her. He said, 'Do you remember the day I took you to our little cemetery? And how the grave next to my parents' grave is where the man who saved my life on the hillside lies ... saved my life by performing a great feat of endurance in getting me back to the station?'

'Yes, yes, I remember it. He died a few weeks later. Because of it, you thought. Of course I remember. I feel that but for him I'd never have met you.'

'Then I'm going to ask you to chalk that up as a good mark for him. He played a hero's part that day. But he was a decidedly shady character, and had always been in and out of trouble with the police. We used to get men like that, hiding away back here, and this one was as crooked as they come. George was sorry for him. He'd been up here years before I came. It was he who'd pinched George's bag of gold when that careless manager left the safe open. Also, one night when he was lying in a drunken stupor, he'd seen young Todd looking over *his* gold. They were both in bank bags, lined. It was very easy to swap them, hide your father's.

Your dad left next day to visit Fairlie and didn't open the bag again. Wiley didn't go with the men when they chased after him, when the loss of George's gold was discovered. He simply said: "That would be what the boy was looking at last night." They went after Todd.

'To them it sounded like a tall story when Todd vowed that that gold wasn't his, that he'd brought it back from his holiday. They had no right to send him off as they did. They should have brought him back to await George's return to sort it out. But it was a bit like the Wild West up here then, with rough justice often being dealt out. But in this case, injustice! My guess is that when the manager discovered the gold was gone they panicked, and were glad enough to find a scapegoat, and not to be suspected themselves!

'Wiley got into a high fever when he was in his last illness and his conscience began to haunt him. George tumbled to it first when he was helping me nurse him. He and Polly had never believed young Todd could be guilty. He'd flayed the men, dressing them down when he came back. Flatly refused to believe it was possible. Said he knew young Todd had gone off for a holiday beyond Skippers, that he could have found gold there.

'Poor Polly—she felt that in his bitterness, Todd could have gone to the bad. That piece of gold George gave you, the squiggly bit, that was part of Todd's gold. It was kept here. George's gold was sold and the proceeds given to an orphanage. You see, Wiley told us where the gold from Skippers was to be found ... under the floorboards in his room. Wiley found a little comfort in the knowledge that he'd saved my life, but it was an unending grief to George and Polly that they were unable to make recompense to Todd. But now they can, quite soon.'

He looked down on her, his eyes tender. 'So there's no barrier any longer to marriage with me. Your father will never forget that you were willing to give me up rather than have him hurt again. That was his great gift to you, heart's darling ... he was willing to face once more the injustice, the disbelief, so you could be happy.'

Juliana was lifting herself towards him, on tiptoe,

aying brokenly, 'Oh, Thor, Thor . . . now I don't have
o hide from you what I feel for you any more. Oh,
Thor, how I've longed to tell you how I love you . . .
you can't imagine how much. Can't even begin to
imagine!'

His lips twitched, 'Oh, but I can. I can.' He put his
hand in his pocket and drew out a piece of crumpled
paper. It had been smoothed out a little. He said,
'Grizel, bless her, asked me to burn up all the
wastepaper basket contents, and a line of this caught
my eye. It says it all:

> *My heart is on the hill with you, man of the mountain*
> *ways,*
> *Where wild and treacherous the storms and filled with*
> *fear my days;*
> *God keep you safe, my love, my own, from harm and*
> *danger free,*
> *Till, when the dragging hours are done, homeward you*
> *come to me.*

'Your father and mother are ringing again in an
hour's time, and they'll be with us in a week. If need be
we'll bring them over the river by helicopter. Oh,
Juliana, isn't it wonderful? We've had so much against
us, till now.'

She nodded. 'Always at cross-purposes. Even in small
things—like you not telling me why you didn't let on
you'd found out I was Fergus Hendrie's daughter.'

Thor laughed. 'By then I was beginning to hope you
might be falling for me, and I was terrified you might
think I wanted you because of that, because it made
you so suitable for here. You could have. Remember
how Anthea, when I said who you were, tried to instil
that very doubt, asked had I drawn up a blueprint for a
high-country wife. I could have choked her!' Juliana
kissed him, said lovingly, 'Idiot!'

A little silence fell. They had said almost everything
that had needed, so desperately, to be said. Thor
gathered her close in an embrace that at last knew no
reserves. Outside the alpine moon shone palely on an
incomparable scene, silver ranges, silver stars, and the

moon itself was as young Todd had written so long
before ... 'at the full, like a jewel' ... he would see
again, the sunsets he had loved, aflame on the snows
the dawnings of coral and rose, the rainbows straddling
the mountains ... and the last vestige of that old
sorrow would be gone. His daughter had given him
that.

Now that daughter lifted her face to that of the man
she loved, the man who had had the courage not to take
no for an answer, who had been confident they
belonged together. Thor's tawny eyes looked deeply
into Juliana's green ones. His fingers were tumbling the
bright hair about her shoulders. His mouth found hers